Praise for Kimberly Raye's
Love at First Bite miniseries

"If you love cowboys and vampires, then
Kimberly Raye's Love at First Bite series is for you."
The Romanorum

"Let's just put this out there…the sex was hot,
incredibly hot. Dare I say Blazin' hot."
—*Bite Club* on *The Braddock Boys: Travis*

"Kimberly Raye's *A Body to Die For* is fun and
sexy, filled with sensual details, secrets and
heartwarming characters—as well as humor
in the most unexpected places."
—*RT Book Reviews*

"*Dead Sexy* by Kimberly Raye is funny
and exciting—with great sex, characters
and plot twists."
—*RT Book Reviews*

"A laugh-out-loud, sexy, heartwarming story
and a wonderful heroine."
—*RT Book Reviews* on *Drop Dead Gorgeous*

"I loved the sexual tension."
—*Night Owl Reviews* on *The Braddock Boys: Brent*

Dear Reader,

I'm thrilled to be back with the latest and final installment in the sexy Braddock Boys series! It's Colton Braddock's turn, and believe me, he's more than ready. Once the brave, courageous leader of *the* most notorious Confederate raiding group during the Civil War, Colton is now a vampire tormented by his past. He's spent over one hundred and fifty years blaming himself for the massacre that killed his son and destroyed his home. No more. He now knows who the real killer is and he's determined to have his revenge once and for all.

His plans are side-tracked, however, when he meets Shelly Lancaster, a strong-willed deputy sheriff with her own agenda. Shelly is tired of reading about hot, mind-blowing sex. She wants to experience it for herself, and so she's on a manhunt to find the perfect partner. When Colton walks into the Skull Creek Sheriff's Office, she knows in an instant that he's just the cowboy for the job.

I hope you've enjoyed riding along with the Braddock Boys these past few books. While I'm saying goodbye to Skull Creek and my beloved cowboy vampires for now, I'll be back in 2013 with a new series featuring the small town of Lost Gun and a trio of wickedly hot brothers named after the most notorious outlaws to ever blaze through Texas!

I love to hear from readers. You can visit me online at www.kimberlyraye.com or write to me c/o Harlequin Books, 225 Duncan Mill Road, Toronto, ON M3B 3K9, Canada, or connect with me on Facebook.

Much love from deep in the heart!

Kimberly Raye

Kimberly
Raye

THE BRADDOCK BOYS: COLTON

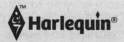

TORONTO NEW YORK LONDON
AMSTERDAM PARIS SYDNEY HAMBURG
STOCKHOLM ATHENS TOKYO MILAN MADRID
PRAGUE WARSAW BUDAPEST AUCKLAND

Recycling programs
for this product may
not exist in your area.

ISBN-13: 978-0-373-79694-6

THE BRADDOCK BOYS: COLTON

Copyright © 2012 by Kimberly Groff

ABOUT THE AUTHOR

USA TODAY bestselling author Kimberly Raye started her first novel in high school and has been writing ever since. To date, she's published more than fifty-eight novels, two of them prestigious RITA® Award nominees. She's also been nominated by *RT Book Reviews* for several Reviewers' Choice awards, as well as a career achievement award. Kim lives deep in the heart of the Texas Hill Country with her husband and their young children. She's an avid reader who loves Diet Dr. Pepper, Facebook, chocolate and alpha males. Kim also loves to hear from readers. You can visit her online at www.kimberlyraye.com or follow her on Twitter.

Books by Kimberly Raye

To get the inside scoop on Harlequin Blaze and its talented writers, be sure to check out blazeauthors.com.

All backlist available in ebook. Don't miss any of our special offers. Write to us at the following address for information on our newest releases.

Harlequin Reader Service
U.S.: 3010 Walden Ave., P.O. Box 1325, Buffalo, NY 14269
Canadian: P.O. Box 609, Fort Erie, Ont. L2A 5X3

This book is dedicated to all of the wonderful readers who love the Braddock Boys as much as I do. You make writing the best job in the world!

1

IT WAS OFFICIALLY the worst moment of her romantic life.

Shelly Lancaster read the singles ad printed in yesterday's edition of the *Skull Creek Gazette* and the Red Bull she'd guzzled at lunch churned in her stomach.

> SWF seeks single, adventurous, incredibly sexy male for hot, mind-blowing sex (no serious relationship wanted). One night only. Instant chemistry a must. For a really good time, email: shellylancaster@skullcreeksheriff.com.

WTF?

Her chest tightened and the air rushed from her lungs. No. No, no, no, no, *no!*

Why had she gone to all the trouble of setting up an anonymous email account—hookmeup@hotmail.com— when no one had even bothered to use it?

Panic bolted through her and she fought for a breath. At least now she understood why her Monday had been straight out of an episode of the *Twilight Zone.*

She should have known something was up. She'd felt the familiar twinge in her gut yesterday. That instinct telling her that something was about to happen.

Something bad. Really bad.

She'd assumed it had something to do with the new prisoner that had been delivered on Saturday. The entire office was on pins and needles because of Jimmy Holbrook. At only twenty-three, he'd built quite a reputation for prison escapes. He'd waltzed out of all four of the facilities where he'd been housed and the Texas Rangers were determined he wouldn't walk out of number five. Hence the transfer to a maximum security prison in El Paso. But in the rush to get him under lock and key at an adequate facility, there had been a few mistakes with his transfer paperwork. Which meant that Jimmy was currently locked up in a back cell awaiting an armed escort to take him the last leg of his trip. Until the paperwork got sorted out, he and the Texas Ranger parked outside his cell were stuck right here in Skull Creek. Hence the churning in her stomach.

Or so she'd thought.

She eyeballed the extra-large container of chocolate body paint sitting on the corner of her desk, a big red bow sitting on top. Justin Wellborn, one of the hottest cowboys to ever two-step across the floor down at the local dance hall, had dropped off the stuff just ten minutes ago and asked her to go back to his place tonight. Before that had been Will Freeman who'd brought a basket of scented massage oils. Kip Walker had come bearing edible underwear and some guy she hardly knew, who worked down at the Dairy Freeze, had shown up with fuzzy zebra-print handcuffs.

They'd all wanted one thing.

Because they thought *she* wanted one thing.

Because the ad that was supposed to protect her identity and list only an anonymous email address had printed the real deal, complete with her name.

Her *name*.

This was *not* happening.

"Big plans tonight?" Sheriff Matt Keller's voice slid into her head and scrambled her thoughts.

She slapped the newspaper closed and whirled. "Just the usual," she blurted, scrambling for a semi-plausible explanation. Anything better than the truth. All she had planned was a glass of wine, a hot bubble bath and a few hours curled up on the couch, watching Bud & Sissy fall madly in love in *Urban Cowboy.* "I'll probably clean my gun or watch whatever game's on ESPN."

"Must be some game." His gaze slid past her to the risqué gifts sitting atop her desk.

"This?" She waved a hand and played on the off chance that Matt had yet to see the personals. "This stuff is for a friend of mine." Her brain raced. "It's for

her, um, party. A bachelorette party." Hey, it sounded
better than what was really happening. *I hate to be
the bearer of bad news, but your number-one deputy
is sexually frustrated and trying to break a three-
year fast.*

Ugh. Matt had enough to worry about. On top
of Holbrook, the town's annual chili cook-off and
roping festival started in less than three days. That
meant parking issues, drunken festival-goers and
lots of litter. She didn't want to add *hormonal female* to the list.

He eyed the items one more time and smiled.
"Good for you. It's nice to see you're having a little fun."

His choice of words punched a nerve and she stiffened. Shelly recalled going to bed hungry one too
many nights because her mother had been too busy
having *fun* to bother making dinner or earning a
steady paycheck. Fun had its price and it wasn't one
she was willing to pay. She liked having food in her
refrigerator and money in the bank and, even more,
peace of mind.

"I'm just collecting the stuff," she blurted, sweeping an arm across the desk and stuffing it all into
her top drawer. "I'm not actually going to the party.
I'm on duty." She slammed the drawer shut. "So, um,
what time does your flight leave in the morning?"
she asked, effectively changing the subject.

"Seven a.m." He glanced at his watch as if he'd
just remembered something. "Hells bells, I need to

get out of here. I promised Shay we'd have a candlelit dinner to kick off tomorrow's trip."

Which was why Shelly was in this mess in the first place.

Instead of worrying about Holbrook or the chili cook-off, Matt was leaving everything to Shelly and running off on a romantic getaway with his new wife.

The man had fallen head over boot heels and was now living the proverbial happily-ever-after. That coupled with the fact that Shelly's younger sister had just spent the past six months planning *the* biggest wedding the town had ever seen, had forced Shelly to re-evaluate her own love life.

Or lack of one.

She was twenty-nine years old. She'd never been married. No kids. No pets. She spent most Saturday evenings either on duty or catching up on paperwork, determined to make something of herself. To be the best. To be someone.

Anyone other than the timid little girl who'd hidden under the bed while her mother had spent her nights down at the local honky-tonk. Shelly had been so scared back then. So helpless.

Never again.

She could outrun, out-throw, outshoot and out arm-wrestle any deputy in the department. With the exception of Buck Kearney, of course, but he had a good two hundred pounds on her. She'd even won Best Throwing Arm during the department's annual softball tournament last year thanks to a little bit of skill, a lot of luck and the fact that the current champion had come down with a stomach bug from eating too many ribs. She was strong-willed. Competitive. Tough. Fearless. At least that's what everyone thought and Shelly had always been more than happy to perpetuate the myth.

Until now.

She wasn't ready to put on her Grandma Jean's lace wedding dress and waltz down the aisle just yet, however. One day maybe. *Hopefully.*

But right now, she had too many responsibilities. She was on the fast track to becoming the first female sheriff of Skull Creek. Matt was retiring in six months to run a bed and breakfast with his new wife, and Shelly wasn't letting anything derail her between now and then.

She didn't want to shed her image and fall in love. She wanted to *make* love. While she'd had a few sexual encounters over the years—in the backseat of Mikey Hamilton's Chevy back in high school and under the bleachers with Casey Lewis during rookie training—they'd been few and far between. She'd had a very limited supply when it came to sex, and she'd never had really good sex.

She wanted one night with a man who stirred the pulse-pounding, do-me-right-now-or-I'll-die chemistry she'd only read about in her favorite romance novels. A few blissful hours to satisfy her starved hormones so that she could stop fantasizing and get back to work.

Not that she was broadcasting that info to the world. She had an image to maintain, which was why she'd placed an *anonymous* ad in the local singles section. Or so she'd thought. Her plan had been to find a man privately—preferably one from any of the surrounding small towns that subscribed to the *Gazette*—and live out the very explicit fantasies heating up her lonely nights. She would have been able to get it out of her system without any of the locals being any the wiser.

Another glance at the paper and her stomach twisted.

"Don't forget the security specialist coming tomorrow for the upgrade." Matt's voice pushed past her pounding heart.

"Tell me again why we need a security upgrade?"

"Because if we had an upgrade, we wouldn't have a Texas Ranger babysitting our prisoner." He motioned to the door leading to the holding area. "The clearance paperwork should be sitting in my email first thing in the morning. Just give him a tour and he'll take care of the rest," Matt tossed over his shoulder as he headed for the door.

The minute the knob clicked, she snatched up the newsprint and signaled to the assistant deputy sitting at a nearby desk.

"Keep an eye on things," she told the man.

"Me?" Bobby Sparks glanced behind him. He

was fresh from the academy and the newest addition to the sheriff's department. Like any good rookie, Bobby didn't so much as wipe his butt without asking permission first. "You're giving me my first assignment?"

Shelly put on her most intimidating face. "Keep your eyes open and don't let anyone past the front desk while I'm gone or else Ranger Truitt will tear me a new one. The holding area is on complete lockdown until Holbrook moves on."

"I'm on it." Bobby's grin spread from ear to ear as he bounced to his feet. "I've been doing simulated fire fights on my Xbox at home. I'm ready for anything."

Oh, boy.

"I'll be back in ten minutes." Shelly stuffed down the worry that roiled inside of her when Bobby paused to check his gun belt. "I'll be on my radio if you need me. And remember, no visitors in the holding area. *No one,*" she reminded him. He could handle this. And even if he couldn't, Beauford Truitt was parked outside Holbrook's cell keeping watch on things.

Everything would be okay.

She tamped down her worry and focused on the task at hand—killing the ad before it became the talk of the entire town.

And then she pushed through the door and headed for the *Skull Creek Gazette*.

"It's Jackson's fault," declared Minerva Peters, the editor-in-chief of the newspaper. "He's our typesetter. Been with the paper going on forty years now. He doesn't see as well as he used to since the cataracts set in. But don't you worry—" Minerva gave her an apologetic smile "—we'll refund your money right away."

"I don't want a refund. I mean…" Shelly's mind raced. "*I* don't want a refund because it's not *my* money. I placed the ad for a friend. You were supposed to use her email, not mine."

Realization seemed to dawn and Minerva smiled. "But of course you did. I knew something was funny about this whole thing. Now if the ad had asked for a female, that I could understand."

"Excuse me?"

Minerva waved a hand. "Don't be shy, honey. I'm the eyes and ears of this town. I know *everything.* Besides, it doesn't take a rocket scientist to figure it out. You never date. You go around dressed like this all the time." She waved a hand at Shelly's uniform. "And you beat up Henry Rogers at the town picnic last year. You obviously butter your bread on the other side just like my niece over in Houston. Why, she came out of the closet just last year and settled down with a cute little hairdresser. Gets free highlights now and everything."

She was not hearing this.

Shelly drew a deep breath and tamped down the anxiety ebbing through her. "First off, this is my uniform. I *have* to wear it. And I didn't beat up Henry. I beat him at arm wrestling, and it was only because he had a pinched nerve." She wasn't sure why she blurted out the truth, but there was just something about the way the woman looked at her—as if she had her completely figured out—that made Shelly want to prove her wrong. "I like men," she heard herself say. "A lot. Just so you know."

"Sure you do." The woman winked as if to say *"It's our little secret."*

All the better, a voice in her head whispered.

That same voice had kept her from telling the entire world that she didn't need the basket of massage oils that had been left on her desk. Not because she wasn't interested in those things, but because she already had her own. She also had chocolate body paint and a pair of fuzzy handcuffs. Pink ones, as a matter of fact. Sure, she'd yet to use them. But still. There was more to Shelly Lancaster than just the rough and tough exterior that everyone saw. She was soft on the inside. Feminine. Just like any other woman.

Just like her mother.

She drop-kicked the thought and eyed Minerva. "I don't want a refund. I want a retraction explaining the mistake."

"No problem. I'll get right on it."

"Great." Relief ballooned in Shelly's chest. "That's the best news I've heard all day."

"Next week," Minerva added, her voice like a pinprick which quickly deflated any relief Shelly had been feeling, "in our very next issue."

"But we need to fix this today." Panic bolted through her. *"Now."*

Minerva shrugged. "We're an itty bitty publication, honey, with a piss poor circulation. Sure, we deliver to the surrounding towns, but their populations are small. We can't afford to put out more than one issue every Sunday."

Which meant the paper would be out there for the world to see for five more days. Her stomach dropped and her eyes burned.

She blinked frantically because no way was she going to start bawling in front of Skull Creek's biggest gossip. Talk about the kiss of death.

"In the meantime," the woman went on, "I wouldn't worry. Hardly anybody is reading print anymore what with that damned internet. Why, Henry Jenkins orders five copies just to line his parakeet cages. And if somebody does actually read it, I'm sure they'll realize we made a mistake." Minerva shook her head. "To think *you* placed an ad like *that?*" The woman shook her head. "Why, it's plum crazy."

"It's not *that* crazy," Shelly blurted before she could stop herself. "I mean, somebody obviously believed it, otherwise I wouldn't have these." She held up the handcuffs as if to say *aha!*

Minerva waved a hand. "There are always a few crazies in the bunch. Testimony to the fact that when men get horny enough, they start to lose brain function. Once those desperate souls open their eyes and realize who they're dealing with, they'll run the other way, honey. Guaranteed."

Gee, thanks.

Shelly ignored the unexpected wiggle of regret and focused on the all-important fact that Minerva was right. No man in his right mind would believe the ad was for real. For the few who did, she would simply set them straight.

News of that would spread well before the newspaper could print a retraction.

A day or two and it would all be over.

She knew that. She just wished it didn't bother her so much.

2

HE WAS WATCHING her again.

Not her, in particular, of course. It was the sheriff's newly arrived prisoner that really got his blood pumping. He'd been hanging around the office for the past three nights now. Watching. Waiting. The female deputy was just an added bonus.

He eyed the beige SUV as it pulled up to the curb out front. The door opened and the driver slid out from behind the wheel. The now familiar brunette walked around the nose of a brown and white Ford Explorer and strode up the steps of the two-story brick building.

The sweet, succulent scent of ripe cherries drifted through the open window of his black Ford F250 pick-up parked across the street. His nostrils flared, his gut clenched and his stomach hollowed out. A wave of awareness rolled through him and he shifted on the leather seat.

It was a crazy-ass reaction considering she barely

looked female with her hair stuffed up under a stiff cowboy hat and her body hidden beneath the drab beige uniform. Reacting to her was friggin' certifiable.

If he'd been your average cowboy.

But Colton Braddock had stopped being a run-of-the-mill wrangler the day he'd drawn his last mortal breath. He was a one-hundred-and-fifty-year-old vampire who fed off both blood and sex, and he was hungry.

Starved.

He watched her pull open the door. Her trousers pushed and pulled, outlining her perfect ass for one delicious moment. His gut tightened. A shiver worked its way up his spine. The uniform, the hard facade, the back-the-hell-up attitude were all just a front for what lay beneath—a soft, curvaceous, passionate woman. Call it instinct. A sixth sense. A vampire's prerogative. Whatever. He *knew* and damned if it didn't work him into a frenzy.

Heat zig-zagged through his body and his heartbeat kicked up a notch. He drew a deep breath. Not that it helped, but old habits died hard, even after an entire century.

Easy.

The command echoed through his head and he drew another breath. And another. While the oxygen didn't sustain him the way it once had, the repetitive motion helped draw his focus away from the demanding need. Watching her was one thing. Touching? Not a chance in hell.

He had plenty of bagged blood stashed back in his suitcase at the motel. More than enough to see him through the next few days while he was stuck in Skull Creek, Texas. While it didn't taste half as good as the fresh stuff, he could make do. He *would* make do. The last thing he needed—the very *last* thing—was to get sidetracked by a woman. Even one that smelled better than a prize-winning cherry pie fresh from the oven.

Not no, but *hell* no.

He'd waited too long for this moment.

For revenge.

The door rocked shut behind her and he forced his attention to the plain brick building.

The jail was a throwback to the olden days with its steel bars on the windows and doors. Appearances aside, he wasn't naive enough to think that the place hadn't been modernized over the years. The sheriff himself was a good friend of Colton's younger brother. The man was also a werewolf. While weres were few and far between and usually at odds with most vampires, Matt Keller was a good man. Trustworthy. He often joined forces with the handful of vampires in town when needed, just as he'd done now.

Once he'd heard the reason for Colton's visit, he'd been more than happy to brief him on the security features that had been installed over the past decade.

An automated lock system. Full camera set-up. Silent alarm. While the local jail wasn't a long-term facility, it was more than adequate to house the average prisoner.

Career criminal Jimmy Holbrook was a completely different story.

The man had been convicted of armed robbery this time and was now sitting inside a cell awaiting transfer to a maximum security prison in El Paso to serve out his sentence.

But it wasn't his crime that had him featured in every newspaper this side of the Rio Grande and a shitload of YouTube videos. It was the fact that he had a "knack" for escaping. At least that's what the media called it.

Colton called it an accomplice.

The sun had set a half hour ago. The overhead spotlights had kicked on, bathing the steps in a soft yellow glow. The place seemed calm. Peaceful. Quiet.

Too quiet for a vampire hell-bent on rescuing her only kin.

While his three brothers felt certain Rose Braddock would come to help her one and only descendant, just as she had time and time again since his first arrest at the age of fifteen, Colton wasn't so sure. She'd turned her back on family once before.

He could still see the billows of black smoke on the horizon and smell the putrid stench of ashes and burned cattle flesh. It had been one hell of a homecoming after four years raiding for the Confederacy. He and his brothers had given Quantrill and his boys a run for their money way back when, but the effort had been wasted. The South had lost and the Braddock boys had headed home to the Circle B to pick up where they'd left off.

He'd ridden up ahead of the others to find what was left of his beloved home, the buildings a smoldering pile of charred wood, the livestock either scattered or dead. And the people...

His throat tightened and bitterness worked its way up. A half-dozen ranch hands had died that night, burned beyond recognition. And the foreman. And his mother. His son. His wife.

Or so he'd thought.

But Rose was alive.

Guilty.

While he had no idea if she'd started the fire herself, he knew she'd played a part. Thanks to his younger brother Cody, they all knew the truth now. Rose hadn't died that night. She'd fled the scene with another man and left them all to perish.

But Colton and his brothers hadn't burned to death. They'd been saved by a vampire, turned just in the nick of time. Garrett Sawyer had happened on the scene by chance and given them another shot at life.

At revenge.

Ironically, he'd bestowed the same gift on Rose. Unknowingly, of course. The ancient vampire never would have turned her if he'd known that she'd practically murdered her family. When he'd run across her a few miles from the scene, he'd thought her and her partner an innocent couple ravaged by savage Indians.

He'd been wrong.

The past stirred along with images from that night. The burning house. A frantic horse. The limp body of a small boy, his face charred so badly he was unrecognizable.

His fingers tightened on the steering wheel. The metal bent, giving way beneath his strength until his prints were permanently indented.

It had been so long since he'd thought of his son. Too long. But with the memory came the pain and so he tucked it back down deep until the pressure inside of him eased. His grip relaxed, but he didn't let go.

Not of the steering wheel, or the anger. He held tight, feeling the heat as intensely as the hunger that now lived and breathed inside of him.

He'd lost everything because of Rose. She was a liar. A traitor. She'd sold him out, which was why his pride hesitated to believe that she would show up now in support of her last living relative. But his head… His head knew the truth.

The pattern was clear. Every reported escape mentioned a visit by a mysterious redhead just prior to the breakout. It *had* to be her.

And if she'd come all those other times, she would come now.

In the meantime…

His gaze shifted to the front window. Through the bars, he watched the deputy pull off her hat and set it on the corner of her desk. Her breasts trembled ever so slightly beneath the stiff blouse, the motion so subtle that he doubted anyone inside even noticed.

He did.

He noticed everything. The slight quiver of her bottom lip. The frantic staccato of her heartbeat. The sweet, succulent aroma of a woman who'd gone far too long without a man.

He fought against a wave of heat, but it was a fight he was destined to lose. He was burning up from the inside out after seventy-two hours cooped up on surveillance. Hungry. Desperate.

For an up close and personal look of the jail, he reminded himself. He'd been biding his time, sleeping during the day and watching all night, waiting for his ticket inside so he could vampire-proof Jimmy's cell in preparation for Rose.

It wouldn't have been a problem if Jimmy had been your average prisoner, but the jail was on lockdown with all deputies on high alert and a ball-busting Texas Ranger parked inside. While Sheriff Matt wanted to help the Braddock boys, he couldn't jeopardize his reputation in the process. Colton needed a believable cover and proper clearance if he wanted access.

Enter Brent Braddock. Colton's brother was an ex-security specialist with friends in high places. He'd managed to get to the right people and pull some strings. Soon Colton would enter the Skull Creek Sheriff's Office as a county-contracted security consultant. His job? To evaluate and perform an upgrade on the current system.

His ticket inside would be ready first thing in the morning and he could quit watching and start doing.

Tomorrow.

He just had to hold out a little longer, bide his time a few more hours. That's what Colton told himself, but damned if he didn't slide from behind the wheel and start across the street anyway.

3

IT WAS TOO QUIET.

Shelly came to that conclusion the minute she sat down at her desk and realized that Bobby was nowhere in sight. Not hunched over his computer or playing video games on his phone or standing in front of the coffeemaker. Her gaze shifted to the men's room.

No doubt the double cheeseburger he'd had at noon had finally caught up to him.

That's what she told herself, but she couldn't shake the strange feeling that something wasn't right. Something besides the local diner's lunch special or the fact that Monty Darlington had left a message on her voicemail asking her if she wanted to get busy back at his place tonight.

Take that, Minerva.

"Bobby?" She tapped on the door. "You okay?"

The only sound that prickled her ears was the steady hum of the air conditioner. She knocked harder. Once. Twice. Her hand tightened on the knob. A loud creak and she found herself inside the one-stall bathroom.

Empty.

Panic sizzled through her for a split-second before she tamped it back down. He was probably out back, talking the hat off the Texas Ranger on duty with Holbrook. Probably shooting the shit and drinking coffee.

She turned toward the containment area, ready to prove her theory when Bobby's voice crackled over the dispatch speakers.

"Mama Bear, this is Baby Bear. You copy?"

A few swift strides, and she punched the button on the microphone. "Would you stop with the nicknames?"

"It's not a nickname. It's code. You never know who might be listening."

"I know exactly who's listening. Martin down at the feed store is the only one with a police band radio and he only tunes in on bridge night to make sure his ex-wife doesn't drink too many mimosas and start streaking again. Where are you?"

"Picking up Honey Gentry. We got a call that she was soliciting outside the Sac-n-Pac," he continued. "They needed a squad car out here asap, so here I am."

"But I told you to stay put."

"And I told him otherwise." The grizzled voice came from behind her and she turned to see her resident Texas Ranger standing in the doorway that led to the cell area.

Rumor had it Beauford Truitt was the oldest Texas Ranger still on active duty and, some said, the toughest. He had snow-white hair, a weathered face and a pickled expression that said he wasn't too happy to be stuck in a one-horse town with Texas's Most Wanted prisoner in tow.

He held a cup of steaming black coffee in one hand and a half-eaten bear claw in the other. "Ain't no sense in him neglecting his duties. Just go on about your business and leave Holbrook to the professionals."

"We *are* professionals."

Yeah right. His expression read loud and clear and Shelly had the fleeting thought that she was in over her head. It was a feeling she'd had many times before when the job had gotten a little too dangerous or her coworkers a little too condescending.

It was a feeling she'd grown all too familiar with growing up with a mother who didn't love her half as much as she loved her social life. All those nights alone had forced Shelly to step up and take care of her little sister when she'd been just a child herself. And while she'd done her best, she'd never managed to shake the uncertainty.

Not that this guy knew that.

She gathered her courage and met his glare head on. "I give the orders here."

"Sure you do, darlin'." He winked. "The prisoner's my responsibility."

"And you're both *my* responsibility, at least while you're in this Sheriff's office." She narrowed her gaze, making it clear she wasn't backing down no matter how many times he called her *darlin'* or *sugar* or *sweetcheeks* or whatever else his *good ole boy* mentality managed to cook up.

Seconds ticked by before he shrugged and she gave herself a mental high five.

"Get some fresh pastries in here before I choke to death," he grumbled, waving the half-eaten goody at her. "This one's as tough as shoe leather." He walked over to the white bakery box sitting next to the coffeemaker and rummaged inside.

Shelly shifted her attention back to the radio. "Finish up and get back here," she told Bobby.

"Yes, ma'am. Baby bear out." The connection ended and Shelly turned toward her desk, her heart still beating double time.

She blew out a deep, easy breath, careful not to let Truitt know that he'd gotten under her skin. She'd come up against his type too many times to count and she knew the worst thing to do was get visibly rattled. It was all about staying calm. In control. Fearless—

The thought faded into the *whoooooooosh* of the front door and the heavy thud of boots.

"I'm looking for Shelly Lancaster," came a deep, masculine voice.

Here we go again.

With Truitt eyeballing her from the coffeemaker, the last thing she needed was a potential suitor carrying another bottle of edible body paint. She had to set the record straight right here and now and put an end to all the nonsense.

"It was a misprint" died a quick death on her tongue when she turned to face off with the man standing in the doorway.

Her heart hitched and all she could do was stare for a long, breathless moment.

He had cowboy written all over him with his straw Stetson and button-down denim shirt. The cuffs had been rolled up to reveal muscular forearms, the tails tucked in at his trim waist. Soft, faded jeans clung to his long legs. A rip in the material gave her a glimpse of one strong, hair-dusted thigh and her throat went dry.

She eyed the scuffed toes of his brown boots before dragging her gaze back up, over his long legs, the hard, lean lines of his torso, the tanned column of his throat, to his face.

Brown hair streaked with the faintest hint of gold brushed his broad shoulders and drew attention to his rugged features. A day's growth of stubble darkened his jaw and outlined his sensuous lips. Blue eyes so pale and translucent they were almost gray collided with hers.

No, it wasn't the way he looked so much as the

way he looked *at her* that sucked the air from her lungs.

"Yes, um, that would be me. At your service," she finally managed to say, her voice breathless and excited and downright giddy.

She stiffened at the realization. No way, no how, would tough-as-nails Deputy Shelly Lancaster let a man—even one as good looking as *this* man—turn her into a pile of quivering Jell-O. She frowned and summoned her most no-nonsense voice. "Is there something I can do for you?"

She had to give him credit. He wasn't the least bit put-off by her tone. Rather, a slow, purposeful grin spread across his face and her stomach hollowed out. "I can certainly think of a few things."

The deep, seductive words echoed in her ears, slipping and sliding along her nerve endings and Shelly knew in an instant that this was it. This was what she'd been reading about. Dreaming of. Searching for.

This was chemistry. Pure and simple.

Potent.

Real.

She enjoyed the heat zinging between them all of five seconds before she gave herself a mental shake that kick-started her common sense. He couldn't know that she'd really been the one who placed the ad. No one could. Which meant she'd better start explaining. And fast.

That's what she told herself, but for a long, heart-pounding moment, she couldn't actually get the words out. There was just something about the way he looked at her, as if he saw every little secret, as if he *liked* what he saw, that stalled the explanation on her tongue.

Instead, she breathed in, drinking in the delicious scent of raw leather and virile male. Electricity hummed through her body and sent tiny shock waves straight to her nipples. Her throat went dry.

"I hate to break up this party," Truitt said, shattering the spell and yanking her back to the here and now and the all-important fact that he'd just witnessed her momentary lapse into desperate female. "But some of us have work to do." A smirk tugged at his mouth as he turned on his heel, coffee cup in hand, and disappeared into the backroom.

She glared after the old man before turning the same look on Mr. Tall, Dark and Yummy. "I don't know you," she finally said, despite the strange inkling that she'd seen him somewhere before. She needed to get back on track. Focused. "And I know everybody in this town."

"The name's Colton Braddock."

She arched an eyebrow. "Any relation to Cody Braddock?" Cody was an ex-bull rider who'd moved to town not long ago. He and his blushing bride were now living happily ever after on the outskirts of town.

"He's my brother."

"You're late. The wedding was two weeks ago."

Something dangerously close to regret flickered in his gaze before fading into those pale, unnerving eyes. "I didn't get the invite in time." He stared at her, into her, and she felt the heat rising up from her feet, whispering through her body and igniting everything in its path. "I've got a cattle spread out in New Mexico. It's a little off the beaten path and the mail isn't what it should be." He shrugged. "But it suits me just fine. I like my privacy."

The words echoed through her head and stirred a completely inappropriate vision of him, the moonlight bathing his naked body as he stood in the middle of a ripe green pasture. He wore the same grin that he was wearing right now and her heart skipped a few beats.

"Privacy is good," she heard herself murmur and his grin widened.

"Oh, it's better than good, sugar." The words stirred another decadent vision and her body trembled. *Trembled,* of all things. It was a reaction straight out of a romance novel. The stuff of fantasies.

But it was real, she reminded herself again.

He was real. And he was here right now.

Thanks to a disastrous misprint.

"I didn't advertise for sex," she blurted, the denial tumbling out before her hormones could block the way.

Surprise gleamed a split second before fading into the pale blue depths of his eyes. A grin tugged at the corner of his mouth. "That's good to know."

"The ad was for a girlfriend of mine," she rushed on. "I placed it for her and the paper accidentally listed my e-mail instead of hers. But if you knew me, you'd know there was no way I would ever do something like that. I'm not the type."

"And just what type are you?" he asked, and she had the distinct feeling that he really wanted to know. That he wanted to know *her*. The fact seemed to startle him if the frown that tugged at his mouth was any indication.

For the first time, she noticed that he wasn't carrying edible undies or massage oils or anything else out of a *Naughty Nights* catalog. Rather, he carried a duffel bag and a clipboard. Realization struck, along with a rush of disappointment.

"You're not here about the personal ad, are you?"

He shook his head. "I'm the private security consultant hired by the county to analyze your current system. I'm sure Sheriff Keller must have mentioned me."

"He did. He also said to expect you tomorrow."

"I finished up my previous job a little early so I thought I'd get a head start." He gave her a disarming smile. "We're not talking any major changes. Just a few added precautions to keep you guys on the transfer schedule with the major prisons. You do take transfers, don't you?"

She nodded. "We had one delivered a few days ago. There was some confusion with his paperwork.

He's sitting here while they sort out the transfer details and then we'll be handing him off to El Paso."

"Perfect. I'll take a look inside, make sure he's safe and secure." His gaze slid past her and for a brief moment, without his full attention fixated on her, she felt a niggle of doubt.

There was something slightly *off* with Colton Braddock. Something she couldn't quite put her finger on.

"It's really late," she heard herself say, "and I've got a lot of loose ends to finish up before my shift ends. Why don't you come back tomorrow? I can show you around then."

"And give you time to check out my credentials?" He arched an eyebrow.

"I have to follow procedure." She shrugged. "I'm sure you understand."

He swept a gaze around the room, seemingly memorizing every detail before his attention shifted back to her, his gaze a brighter shade of blue this time, and she forgot what she was about to say.

Instead, she found herself wondering what he would taste like. Sweet and intoxicating and addictive? Dark and dangerous and forbidden? All of the above?

And then some.

The sound of his voice floated through her head, but his lips didn't move. Instead, they tilted in a sensuous grin that did wicked things to her self control. Her hands trembled and her mouth watered.

She wanted to kiss him so badly.

And he wanted to kiss her.

She could see it in the way his eyes darkened and the muscle in his jaw twitched. He wanted to close the distance between them. Just a few feet and bam, they'd be toe-to-toe.

Touching.

Kissing.

"Tomorrow it is," he murmured. And then, just like that, he vanished. No creak of the door. No click of the knob. Nothing. It was as if he'd disintegrated into thin air.

As if.

She'd been on the job for twelve hours straight, pulling a double shift yet again to prove to Matt that she was more than capable and dedicated. She was starting to get punchy. That was the reason she hadn't seen him turn and walk away. Even more, it explained the crazy disappointment whispering through her.

A kiss?

Seriously?

She hardly knew him and he hardly knew her. Even more, she wasn't going to get to know him because he was only here to tweak their security system. It was business and everyone knew that the town's first female deputy didn't mix business with pleasure.

No matter how hot he was or how sexually frustrated she was.

Rather, she was going to go home just as soon as Bobby got back, drown her troubles in a hot bath and get some much-needed sleep before she came face-to-face with Colton Braddock first thing in the morning.

Until then...

She walked over to the box of pastries, unearthed a chocolate-covered donut and took a big bite. The sugar melted in her mouth, sending a rush of satisfaction through her, albeit a temporary one. They weren't *that* stale. At least not to a desperate, deprived woman.

It wasn't sex, but it was definitely the next best thing.

4

COLTON CLIMBED BEHIND the wheel of his truck and tried to figure out what the hell had just happened.

He'd tried to glamour her and it hadn't worked. Not a lick.

Sure, she'd looked as if she'd *wanted* to fall under his spell with her parted lips and her smoldering eyes and her *take me now* vibe. She'd even leaned toward him once or twice, as if she meant to give in to the pull and cross the room. But then...

Nothing.

Not a damned thing.

She hadn't launched herself into his arms and begged him to come closer, to make himself right at home.

Hell, no. She'd stood her ground and told him to come back tomorrow.

Tomorrow.

If he hadn't been so irritated, he might have actually smiled. It had been a long time—over one hundred and fifty years to be exact—since a woman had faced off with him and actually won.

Women typically melted at his feet when he looked into their eyes. Not that he was proud of that fact.

It was simply the nature of the beast that he'd become and, he had to admit, it had its advantages. He didn't have to worry about showing his true nature when he was having sex. All he had to do was stare deeply into his partner's eyes and will away her memory of him.

But there was too much riding on this moment and he needed inside of that jail too badly to be the least bit amused right now. Or turned on. He needed Shelly's cooperation more than he needed her luscious body.

The thought struck and conjured all sorts of images and he damned himself for thinking with his dick. But that, too, was the nature of the beast.

He wanted her the way he wanted all women.

Okay, so he wanted her a little bit more. She was more sexually frustrated than the average female which meant she had all that sweet, succulent energy bottled up inside of her, just waiting to be unleashed. That made her all the more attractive and damned if he didn't want to peel away her stiff exterior and see the delicate curves hiding beneath.

Hiding. That's what she was doing.

He knew because he'd been doing it himself for

more years than he could count. Living in the shadows, protecting his true nature, surviving.

For revenge.

That's the reason he'd kept going all those years ago when he'd lost everything. The reason he kept going now. He'd dreamt of payback, lusted after it, and now was his chance to have it.

He didn't have time for some stubborn female with a badge. No time for touching or kissing.

Especially kissing.

He played the scenario over and over in his head for the next few minutes. The desperate urge to cross the distance to her, lean forward and touch his lips to hers.

To distract her. Persuade her.

It certainly hadn't been because he'd *wanted* to kiss her. Sex was one thing. It was all about survival. Sustenance. But kissing? Talk about personal. Colton had no intention of getting personal with any woman.

No matter how much he suddenly wanted to.

"There's no reason to sit out here all night."

The deep voice shattered his train of thought, thankfully, and he turned to see his brother slide onto the seat next to him.

"She's not even close." Brent Braddock closed the door and eyed his older brother. "So why don't you give it up and come home with me? Abby really wants to spend some time with you."

Colton arched an eyebrow. "Abby, huh?"

Brent shrugged. "Okay, so maybe I wouldn't mind

catching up myself." He met Colton's gaze. "I know Cody and Travis wouldn't mind it either. In fact, Cody really wanted you to stay out at his place."

"The hotel is working just fine." Or it would be if the eightysomething-year-old woman who ran the place with her grandson would stop banging on his door throughout the day, wanting to change his sheets.

"Suit yourself, but it seems a shame not to take advantage of the fact that we're all together."

"We're here for a reason."

"She won't show up for a few more days at least," Brent reminded him. "My contact at the prison did the transfer really fast and on the fly. Holbrook isn't due in El Paso until the day after tomorrow. If Rose has already figured out he's being moved—and that's a big *if*—she'll be waiting there for him. Add twenty-four hours for her to trace the transfer and identify exactly where he's been delayed once she figures out that something is up. Another twenty-four for her to reach Skull Creek since she can only travel at night. That means we've got at least a week to sit around and wait." He caught Colton's stare. "I can't think of a better way to spend it than getting re-acquainted with each other."

"I'd rather not take any chances."

Brent looked as if he wanted to argue, but then he shrugged. "Suit yourself." He opened the passenger door and paused. "I could hang out here for a little while."

"Go home to your wife."

"You shouldn't have to do this by yourself."

"But I'm going to." Colton met his brother's gaze. "This is my fight, not yours. You know that." While they'd all suffered thanks to Rose, Colton had suffered the most. He'd lost everything and he would be the one to make her pay.

Brent looked as if he wanted to object, but then he nodded. "If you change your mind about tonight, we'll be at my place." In the blink of an eye, he was gone and Colton settled back in his seat to keep watch.

At least, he tried to settle in. But his nerves were wound too tight, his hands clenched, his gut tense.

Not because of Rose. Brent was right about one thing—she wasn't even close. Colton could sense other vampires and while he felt the steady hum from his brothers and the others in Skull Creek, that was it. No prickling up his spine. No tingling in his limbs. No spike of anger in his gut.

Yet.

But she would come eventually and he would have his pound of flesh. That would be the end of it.

The end of him.

Because this wasn't just about defeating Rose. It was about punishing her for what she'd done, and then paying the price himself for not preventing it in the first place.

That's why he'd come here.

Skull Creek would be the end. Of Rose and of the damnable guilt that ate away inside of him.

Until then…

The scent of ripe cherries teased his nostrils. His mouth watered and his gut twisted and he stiffened.

He was in for a long night.

SHELLY WAS ON HER third donut when Bobby arrived with a tall, tanned blonde in tow.

"I wasn't soliciting," Honey Gentry said as the deputy steered her into a chair. "I was advertising."

Although well into her late thirties, the woman didn't look a day over twenty-five. With long, dark blond hair and a figure that would make any Dallas Cowboys Cheerleader insanely jealous, Honey was the sort of woman who turned heads when she walked into any room. Especially wearing skimpy Daisy Duke shorts that accented her long, endless legs and a red tank top that outlined her perfect breasts. Add a pair of red cowboy boots and it was no wonder she'd caused a riot at the Sac-n-Pac.

"Thank God. Finally I can talk to someone who doesn't think with his crotch." Heavily lined cornflower blue eyes shifted to Shelly. "This is all a big misunderstanding."

Shelly arched an eyebrow. "I thought you promised Judge Myers that you were going to turn over a new leaf if he let you off with probation last year?"

"I swear I didn't do anything."

"Not yet." Bobby handed over a hot pink flyer. "I

caught her just in time. She was handing out these. Gave one to the mayor's wife. She's the one who called it in."

"Pinkie Hamilton is as nutty as a squirrel turd. She's just mad 'cause her husband is one of my best customers." Honey beamed. "He loves my honey buns."

"You might want to keep that info to yourself until you talk to a lawyer," Shelly warned.

"I was just advertising my product. That isn't against the law."

"It is if the product is a sexual favor."

"It's not a sexual favor." Honey beamed. "I've expanded from breakfast pastries," she indicated the basket that Bobby had plopped on Shelly's desk, "to cupcakes. It's my new business. I'm a cupcake caterer."

"Yeah, right." Bobby snorted and glanced at the pink flier. "You're trying to tell us that *Decadent Thunder Down Under* is the name of a cupcake?"

"One of my top sellers." Honey flicked her long mane of hair. "And it's the mayor's personal favorite which is why his wife hates my guts. She can't cook a lick." She motioned to the basket. "I've got a half dozen to deliver to him. He got stuck in a late meeting so I thought I'd do a little advertising at the Sac-n-Pac until he finished." She motioned to the basket of sweet-smelling goodies. "It's my granny's recipe."

"Cupcakes, huh?" Shelly eyed the list. "Chitty Cherry Bang Bang and Lickety My Banana Split," she read out loud and her gaze shifted to Honey. "Don't you think those names might be misconstrued?"

"It's called suggestive branding. I learned it on the internet." The woman shrugged. "It ain't my fault if this whole town's got their minds in the gutter. I'm just trying to beef up my business."

"Well you're out of business for now," Bobby informed her as he slid behind his desk and reached for an arrest sheet.

"For soliciting?" Shelly asked the deputy.

Bobby shook his head. "When I told Pinkie I couldn't arrest someone just because of a flyer, she got the owner of the Sac-n-Pac to file charges for loitering."

"But that's not fair," Honey protested. "I wasn't loitering. I was an actual customer. I even bought a large sweet tea and a bag of Doritos before I started handing out flyers."

"Tell it to the judge." Bobby reached for his fingerprint kit while Shelly barely resisted the urge to put a stop to the nonsense.

"I'm sure Judge Meyers will throw it out in a heartbeat," she told Honey. "But we have to go through the motions when anyone presses charges."

"This sucks." Honey blew out an exasperated breath. "I'm going to miss *Lost*."

"Maybe not." Shelly made a mental note to get Bobby to move the small television from the back room into Honey's cell. Yes, it violated about ten different rules, but this was a small town and these were trumped up charges. Tit for tat.

She gave Honey an encouraging smile and settled down behind her desk to finish up her own paperwork.

Her thoughts kept going to Colton Braddock and the all important fact that out of all the men who'd crossed her path that day, he'd turned out to be The One. Also known as the answer to her sexually frustrated prayers. Which wouldn't have been such a bad thing except he wasn't here because he wanted to have a little fun. He was here to do a job.

And he was coming back tomorrow.

She stiffened and eyed the basket sitting on the corner of her desk. Icing clung to the edge of the lid and the warm scent of sugar and vanilla teased her nostrils. The trio of donuts she'd had hadn't come close to touching the hunger that gnawed inside of her. She needed something more filling.

She needed him.

Shelly shook away the sudden thought and leaned forward. Her hand was an inch shy of the basket when the door buzzed open and a redhead wearing a pair of oversize sunglasses rushed inside.

"Hide me," said Shelly's younger sister.

"Sunglasses? Really? It's seven o'clock in the evening."

"I don't want to be recognized." As if that would ever happen. At twenty-three, Darla Lancaster was tall and leggy with a killer body and enough sex appeal to have all the men in town chasing after her. She'd slowed down long enough to let one in particular catch up, only to leave him at the altar three days ago with no explanation. She'd been avoiding him ever since.

"Billy Spoon saw me coming out of the Iron Horseshoe about ten minutes ago," Darla said, breathless. "I'm sure he's on the phone right now blabbing to Tom." Tom was the man she'd stood up at the altar. He was also a high powered lawyer and the mayor's son. Translation? He had connections. Lots of them. "I'm not ready to see him yet."

"You left him high and dry in front of a church full of people. You left *me* high and dry in front of a church full of people." Wearing the worst dress *ever*, she added silently. "Don't you think you owe him an explanation?" While the wedding planner had told everyone that the bride had had a family emergency, there'd been no further details as to why the lavish event had been cancelled. Nothing but an "I'm sorry" and "Be sure to pick up a slice of cake for the road."

"How can I explain what happened when I don't even know?" Darla rushed to the window, slid the sunglasses down her nose and peeked past the blinds. "He's rich. Handsome. Nice. *Perfect*." She turned a confused expression on Shelly. "I left the perfect man at the altar. What's wrong with me?" Before Shelly could respond, she added, "He sent me flowers today. Imported Italian tea roses. Only the best for the best." Her eyes filled with tears. "That's what the card said. Talk about a great guy, right? Tom can give me everything I've ever wanted. Even the sex is good." Her gaze collided with Shelly's. "So why don't I love him?"

"Love is overrated." Shelly had learned that first-hand after watching their mother fall in love over and over again. "Settle for good sex and consider yourself lucky."

"I can't marry him if I don't love him. But if I blow him off, he'll get really mad and then he won't *want* to marry me. Then what if I change my mind and decide I *do* want to marry him?" She shook her head. "I just need to stay out of sight while I try to figure things out. That way I keep my options open."

"That's the most ridiculous thing I've ever heard."

Even more ridiculous, it made sense. At least where Darla was concerned.

Shelly and her sister had grown up on the wrong side of the tracks with little money and few choices. With their mother out kicking up her heels every Saturday night and most nights in between, they'd been left to fend for themselves. Alone. Scared. Uncertain.

Shelly had overcome that uncertainty by working her way through the police academy and joining the Sheriff's department. Her baby sister had done it with makeup and hair extensions. While Shelly could outshoot any man in Skull Creek, Darla could have him eating out of her hand with one sultry smile.

"My shift ended a few hours ago. Bobby can stall him if he comes in while I drop you off on my way home." She motioned to the rear of the jail. "My car's out back."

Darla grinned. "You're the best big sister in the world."

"Remember that the next time you're tempted to force me into a hideous bridesmaid's dress."

"That dress was straight off a Paris runway, not that you would know that, since the last time you actually went dress shopping was—I don't know—*never*. Speaking of which—" She eyeballed her sister. "—since you're going to bite the bullet and find yourself a man, you might want to fix yourself up a little." She stared at Shelly's starched brown cover-everything-up uniform. "Your wardrobe needs sexing up in the worst way."

"My wardrobe is just fine the way it is and the newspaper made a mistake. It wasn't my ad."

Darla smiled. "I knew it! I told Mom that it had to be a misprint, but she thinks you've finally lightened up and are now following in her footsteps."

She glared at her sister. "Just meet me out back."

5

SHELLY WASN'T SURE what bothered her more—seeing Colton Braddock still parked outside the jail at midnight when she'd come back after dropping her sister off. Or the zing of excitement she felt at finding him there.

He sat behind the wheel of his black Ford pickup, his window down, his hat tipped low, his attention fixed on the building directly across the street.

She eased her Mustang up behind him and killed the engine. A few seconds later, she leaned into the open passenger window of his truck. "Nice night."

He didn't so much as glance at her. Instead, his eyes stayed fixed on the jail. "Nice enough."

"You usually start most of your assignments with a stakeout?"

"I like to get a feel for a place before I go in."

"And what's your feel for this place?"

He shrugged one broad shoulder and she had the

same sense of déjà vu that had come over her when he'd first stepped inside the jail.

As if she'd seen him somewhere before.

Duh. You've seen his brother. There has to be a family resemblance.

Probably.

"Typical small town set-up." His voice killed any further speculation and drew her full attention. "Front office. Rear containment area. Two or three cells at the most. Good when it comes to a few drunks and the occasional bar fight. Not so good for a prisoner like Holbrook."

"You're here because of him, aren't you?"

"Maybe."

"Either you are or you aren't." She watched him watch the building. "So which is it? Did the county send you in because they don't think we can handle it?" That *I* can handle it? "Or is this all just a coincidence?"

Her instinct was telling her it was number one. Still, she couldn't help but hope she was wrong.

He didn't seem in any hurry to put her out of her misery. Seconds ticked by before he leaned across the cab and grabbed the door handle. The latch clicked and the door opened.

"Get in and I'll tell you." Challenge gleamed hot and bright in his gaze.

Shelly had never been one to shy away when called out. That, and she suddenly couldn't help herself. While her brain told her to run like hell, her hormones were like heat-seeking missiles and Colton Braddock was a blazing inferno. She climbed in.

Leather shifted as she settled on the seat. Hinges creaked and the door closed with a thud. The rich aroma of sexy male surrounded her, pushing and pulling at her already tentative control. The urge to slide across the seat and cozy up nearly overwhelmed her. It had been so long since she'd felt a man next to her.

Even more, she'd never felt one like Colton Braddock.

An air of sensuality clung to him, as if sex was as natural to him as breathing. The musky scent of leather and male filled the cab, teasing her senses and making her heart flutter. The air between them crackled with electricity.

The chemistry was potent, but she wasn't about to give in to it. The last thing she needed was for him to report back to the county that she was anything but professional. This was her job. Her future. And so she gathered her strength and her composure.

"So which is it?" she asked again. "Are you a babysitter for Big Brother? Because if that's the case, you can head right back to Austin and tell them thanks, but no thanks. I'm more than capable of handling anything that happens here."

"Holbrook is a lot more dangerous than you realize."

"I'm fully aware of his background. I've got two deputies on him right now." John had reported in minutes before she'd left with Darla. "And I'll be back first thing in the morning to keep an eye on things myself. Trust me, he's not going anywhere."

"I'm sure that's what they said at the last four facilities he escaped from." His gaze sparked and the twelve inches of leather that separated them seemed to shrink. Colton half turned toward her, resting one arm across the back of the seat, his hand an inch shy of touching her. "So did you check out my story?" His gaze caught and held hers for a long, heart-pounding moment.

"I texted the Sheriff," she said, staring past him at the front of the jail. "But I don't expect a reply back right away because he's officially on vacation. He and his wife are going on a trip."

"Which means I'm not getting in until tomorrow."

She nodded. "If you are who you say you are." She wasn't sure why she said it. His story fit and she had no real reason to doubt it. There was just something odd about him.

Not in a bad way. Just…different.

Exciting.

She squelched the thought and concentrated on breathing.

"What makes you think I'm lying?"

She shrugged and met his gaze head on. "I just get the feeling there's more to you than meets the eye."

SHE HAD NO IDEA.

The thought shot through Colton's head as he

stared at the woman sitting next to him. Long, dark tendrils had come loose from her ponytail and lay limp and forgotten against her creamy neck. Heat rolled off her, teasing his senses, and it was all he could do to keep from brushing his fingertips across her skin. He was so close. Too close. "Maybe there's more to *you* than meets the eye," he said instead.

Her gaze narrowed and he had the sneaking suspicion that she was trying to intimidate him. "What's that supposed to mean?"

"Maybe you aren't half as tough as you want everyone to think." He didn't miss the faint tremble of her bottom lip before her mouth pulled into a tight frown.

"You don't know anything about me."

"Then tell me something."

"I could kick your ass fifty ways til Sunday if I felt like it."

He grinned, the expression coaxing the tiniest of smiles from her. The sudden tension between them eased just a little. "On a good day, maybe."

"On any day."

His grin widened. "So how long have you been a Deputy Sheriff here?"

"Six years. Before that, I did a few years on patrol in a nearby county."

"That's a long time in a tough field. No wonder you're so prickly."

"Very funny." She eyed him. "What about you? How long have you been a security specialist?"

"Not very long." He didn't miss the questions swimming in her gaze. "The ranch isn't earning what it used to and I needed to make ends meet. My brother runs a security firm, so he hooked me up."

"Who looks after things at your place while you're away?"

"I've got a reliable foreman and a few steady hands. It makes turning my back a lot easier." At least that's what Colton had been telling himself since he rolled into Skull Creek to face off with Rose. He didn't have to worry about his animals back in New Mexico. Jasper and the boys would take care of them. Hell, they'd be tickled pink when they found out that Colton had left them each an equal share of his land.

It's not like he would be needing it.

There was no going back after this. No putting the past behind him and settling down. No finding happiness the way his brothers had.

His happiness had died that night right along with his son. He had no illusions about getting over the loss. Killing Rose would give him some sense of satisfaction, but it wouldn't rid him of the damnable guilt. He would never be free. He didn't deserve to be free.

"So you're not married?" her soft voice pushed into his thoughts and eased the sudden tension that had gripped him.

His gaze met hers. *No* was right there on the tip of his tongue, but damned if he could get the word out. "I was once," he heard himself say instead. "A long time ago. But it didn't work out."

"Kids?"

"One. A long time ago. That didn't work out either." When she seemed puzzled, he added, "He passed away."

"I'm really sorry," she murmured and he knew by the brightening in her eyes that she wasn't just being polite. She meant it.

So? Her sympathy didn't change anything. Not the past. Or the future.

Still, he felt the knot in his chest ease just a little.

"What about you?" he asked her. "Do you have a husband tucked away somewhere?" As if he didn't already know. She was too sexually deprived to have a steady guy waiting at home. But he asked anyway because he liked the sound of her voice. "Kids?"

"I'm much too busy to be a wife and mother. Especially a mother." She stiffened as soon as the words rolled out and he knew she'd said more than she'd meant to.

He held her gaze, trying to delve into her thoughts, wanting to for the first time in a long time, despite the nagging voice that told him to *back the hell up.* He didn't need the distraction.

But damned if he didn't want one.

Colton was sick of waiting. Of watching the clock while the minutes dragged on and he grew more and more anxious. He needed some way to fill his time and talking with her suddenly seemed harmless enough.

He eyed her. "You sound like you speak from personal experience."

"My own mother wasn't the most attentive."

"Did she work too much?"

"She played too much. She had no time leftover for anything else, especially me and my sister. It was no big deal." She shrugged. "We managed just fine without her." A smile tugged at her lips. "I learned to make a mean peanut butter and jelly sandwich."

"What about your dad?"

"I never really knew him. He was more of a Saturday night special than marriage material."

"Marriage is overrated."

She eyed him. "Now you sound like the one speaking from personal experience."

"I was the oldest and itching to settle down and carry on the family name, and she was itching to get away from her bastard of a father. It seemed like the right thing to do at the time." But he'd been wrong. Dead wrong. "My son was the only good thing to come out of it." An image of CJ sitting atop his first horse flashed in Colton's mind and he felt a smile tug at his lips.

"What happened to him?"

The question hit like a two-by-four and he remembered that night. The smoke. The blood. The death.

His muscles went tight and his gaze zeroed in on her. "Why did you place an ad for sex?" The quick change of subject caught her off guard and he saw the panic that flashed in her expression.

"I didn't."

"Yes, you did. Otherwise you wouldn't be so dead set on denying it."

Her mouth drew into a tight line. "It's late." She reached for the door handle. "You should call it a night and head back to the hotel."

"Settle down." He touched her then, his hand closing over her shoulder. "There's no reason to get fired up. I don't bite." A grin tugged at his lips. "Not unless you ask real nice."

What the hell was he doing?

He was flirting. Friggin' *flirting*. And damned if he could help himself. He liked seeing the color rush to her cheeks and the sharp intake of her breath. She was nervous and he got the feeling that such a thing didn't happen very often where Shelly Lancaster was concerned.

"If you know what's good for you, you'll move your hand."

"And if I don't?"

"I'll move it for you." That's what her mouth said, but her body wanted something altogether different. Heat rolled off her in waves and she trembled with need. A need she fought with everything she had. Emotion warred in her expression. Desire versus aggravation. Desperation versus full-blown anger.

Forget warm and willing and ready like every other woman he'd come into contact with. She was different, and damned if that didn't draw him more than if she'd stripped off her clothes and planted herself on his lap.

The seconds ticked by and he willed her closer.

She didn't budge and his frustration built.

If she wouldn't give in to the chemistry raging between them, he would just have to do it himself.

Quick and fiery. That's what he told himself as he leaned down and captured her mouth with his own. A fast and ferocious kiss just to satisfy his curiosity and see if she tasted half as good as she looked.

Better.

Her lips were warm and sweet, and in that next instant, there seemed nothing wrong with slowing down just a little and taking his time.

His tongue tangled with hers and he slid his arms around her waist. He pulled her close, his mouth eating at hers, tasting, exploring, *drinking.*

The notion struck as he felt the first wave of energy shimmer through his body. It spilled from her lips, feeding him for a few blissful moments before the shock of what was happening hit him hard and fast.

A climax was one thing, but this was just a kiss. He shouldn't feel such a rush. No heat pouring into him, feeding the coldness inside. No burst of sweet, blissful energy.

"No!"

The protest rang loud and clear in his head. Not his own, though his conscience was rioting pretty loudly at the moment. Rather, the *no* came from her and sent a bolt of common sense streaking through him. He pulled away, cutting off the addictive stream of energy and breaking the connection between them.

Her eyes popped open and she stared up at him. Shock flashed in her gaze, along with a glimmer of disappointment before she seemed to gather her self-control.

Her eyes narrowed. "Good try, but you're still not getting into the jail before the morning." And then she opened the door and climbed out. "Pack it up and get out of here. You're violating curfew."

"You've got to be kidding?"

"Hazards of a small town." She slammed the door shut and stepped back onto the curb. "Now move before I write you a ticket."

She glared and Colton knew beyond a doubt that she had every intention of following through on her threat. He stared at her a moment longer, willing her one last time to weaken, to crawl back into the truck and beg for another kiss, but she didn't budge.

She was a strong one. He had to give her that. And double damned if he didn't like that about her, too.

He frowned and keyed the engine. "I'm not much of a morning person. I'll be in tomorrow evening. Six o'clock." And then he did what he should have done the moment she pulled up behind him—he hauled ass in the opposite direction.

HE'D KISSED HER.

Even worse, she'd kissed him back.

The truth needled Shelly as she watched his tail-lights disappear around the corner.

She'd kissed him back despite every ounce of common sense that had screamed she was being crazy. She knew good and well that he was just trying to wiggle his way into the jail a few precious minutes early. The kiss had been a distraction, a way to shatter her defenses and get his way.

Bingo.

She ignored the know-it-all voice and focused on the short drive to her house and the lucky fact that while she'd kissed him back—and wow what a kiss—no one had actually seen her do it. It was his word against hers if he decided to tell the world that there was more to Shelly Lancaster than met the eye.

Much more.

He wouldn't. While he had no trouble calling her out face-to-face, she had the feeling that Colton Braddock was too much of a man to kiss and tell.

Which meant she had only her own conscience to worry about.

She ignored the sinking feeling that she'd made a huge mistake. That one kiss would lead to another. And another. And—no!

She'd been weak, yes, but only because she'd pulled two shifts back-to-back. A hot bath and some much needed sleep and she would surely stop acting like a sex-starved lunatic.

Hopefully.

6

OKAY, SO MAYBE a bath wasn't the best idea after the red hot kiss with Colton Braddock.

Shelly admitted as much an hour later as she peeled off her clothes and sank down into the warm water. Her lips still tingled from his kiss and her nerves buzzed. The heady scent of her favorite bubble bath filled the air and her senses were wide open and raw as she slid the bath sponge over her sensitive skin.

Don't think it.

Her fingers tightened on the sponge an inch shy of her nipple and she caught her breath. She needed to stop obsessing over sex. Block it from her mind. Forget it. *Forget him.*

So what if he was handsome and sexy and they had explosive chemistry? So what if he'd kissed her and she'd kissed him back? He wasn't some anonymous horn dog from a nearby town. He was a colleague, at least for the next few days, which meant she had to keep things purely platonic between them.

Professional, as in no kissing.

Although, maybe if she obsessed just a little in the privacy of her own home now, enough to have one teeny, tiny orgasm, it might ease the knot of frustration so she could actually remember not to kiss him later.

Hey, it was worth a shot.

She touched the sponge to the tip of her nipple and a gasp bubbled past her lips. It wasn't the real thing, but it would do.

She swirled the fragrant soap around the sensitive tip. First one then the other. Delicious tingles danced across her nerve endings. Her lips parted on a gasp as she moved her hands lower, down the silken plane of her belly. Her legs parted and her fingers slid even lower.

Her breathing grew faster, her chest heaving as her fingers parted the silky folds between her thighs. But it wasn't her own hand doing the touching. It was his.

In her mind's eye, she saw Colton Braddock, felt his purposeful touch against her moist heat, his long, deft fingers sliding deep to wring a shudder from her.

Once. Twice. Again.

Sensation exploded, sweeping across her nerves like a brushfire. Only when she'd taken a deep breath, her trembling hands grasping the tub's edge, did she hear the voice.

"I told you I wouldn't bite." The deep, rich voice slid into Shelly's ears, to stir her senses back from their temporary exhaustion.

She drank in a slow, steadying breath and lifted her heavy lids. Through the steam, she saw him standing in the bathroom doorway, his powerful body filling up the small room. He wore the same faded jeans he'd had on earlier, but he'd slipped off his shirt. Muscles gleamed and flexed in the dim light. A pair of matching slave band tattoos encircled his bulging biceps. His eyes pulsed a hot, bright, brilliant purple.

"This isn't real." Her own voice sounded soft and subdued and oh, so far away. She must be imagining things. That's why his eyes were purple now, not pale blue.

She'd finished off two glasses of wine before crawling into the tub. Add to that the sugar extravaganza she'd indulged in at work and it was a wonder she wasn't seeing little green men or even the Easter Bunny.

She pushed to her feet, water drip-dropping all around her as she stepped from the tub. Her heart pounded and the air seemed to thicken with need.

"You aren't really touching me." She moved trembling fingers to her breast. "I'm doing this all by myself." She held his gaze, her fingertips swirling around the tip until it hardened and throbbed and her throat went dry. "And this." She delivered the same careful attention to the other breast.

A battle raged across Colton's features, as if he wanted to reach out but couldn't.

After all, this was *her* fantasy. He could only do as she commanded, and right now she was too busy enjoying the moment to beckon him forward. She liked having him watch. For now.

Her breath caught as she trailed her hands down to the silky strip of hair at the base of her thighs. She followed the sensitive flesh to the slit between her legs. The tip of her finger eased in just a fraction and sensation drenched her. Her eyes closed and her heart rate quickened.

"Holy hell."

His deep voice pushed past the haze of pleasure and echoed in her head. Her eyes fluttered open.

"You're beautiful," he said, even though his lips didn't move, proving once more that she was caught in a very vivid, very erotic fantasy. One that was just getting started.

"Touch me," she finally breathed.

Without breaking eye contact, he closed the few feet between them and dropped to his knees, bringing his head level with her waist. Silky hair brushed her bare stomach.

Impossible.

But in the thick, steamy fog of the bathroom, it was more than plausible. She felt the rough stubble of his jaw against her abdomen, saw the tremble of his shoulders as he leaned forward, felt the flutter of his lips against her skin.

Fire exploded and she tilted her head back. A moan sailed past her parted lips.

"I like touching better than watching." His deep voice echoed in her head at the same time his tongue darted out, licking and dipping at her navel.

Her legs went weak. She grasped his shoulders, her fingers digging into the hard, carved muscle as his lips worked magic on her skin. His tongue caught the diamondlike drops of water that slid down her flesh and her heart beat a frenzied rhythm against her rib cage.

Oxygen bolted from her lungs when his tongue parted the sensitive flesh between her legs. His shoulders pushed her legs apart until she stood completely open and eager and then he devoured her.

He thrust his tongue deep and drank in her essence. She went wild. Heat drenched her. She bucked and her body convulsed and he lapped at her as if he'd never tasted anything so sweet.

He swept her into his arms and a heartbeat later she felt the soft mattress at her back.

"More," she heard herself say when he pulled away this time. She wanted to be embarrassed at the desperation in her voice. Begging, of all things. But this was just a fantasy. An erotic escapade where pleasure took priority over pride. "Don't go."

"I'll be back, sugar. That's a promise."

COLTON FORCED ASIDE the image of Shelly and opened his eyes to the dimly lit motel room. An ancient ceiling fan trembled above him, the blades moving in a lazy circle that barely stirred the stifling summer air. Awareness rippled up and down his arms and he felt the frantic pounding in his chest. Her heartbeat.

No way. No friggin' *way*.

They'd shared one kiss. Sure, it had been a pretty spectacular kiss, but still. That wasn't the way it worked. He had to drink a substantial amount from her to forge a real connection.

A kiss wasn't enough. It never had been in all the years he'd been a vampire and it sure as hell wasn't now.

That's what he told himself, but there was no denying the sweet scent of bubble bath that clung to him or the ripe taste of her luscious sex that lingered on his tongue. He'd been there tonight, all right.

In spirit.

Which meant his damned body was still as hungry as ever. More so now that he'd had a taste of what he so desperately wanted. He needed to feed—*really* feed—in the worst way.

He pushed to his feet and unearthed the small cooler from the bottom of his suitcase. Pulling out a bag of AB-, he headed for the small microwave that sat next to the scarred dresser. A minute later, he dumped the warm liquid into a glass and touched the rim to his lips. The sweet heat rolled down his throat, but it wasn't enough to fill up the emptiness in the pit of his stomach.

It was never enough.

He slammed the thought and took another gulp just as the doorknob trembled. His gaze shifted and he realized a split-second too late that he'd forgotten to secure the door. He crossed the room in a flash and caught the knob just as it turned.

"Turn down service," came the old woman's voice.

"I'm good." Colton pressed the door closed and flipped the lock.

"But I've got free mints for your pillow."

"I'll pass." He reached for a nearby desk chair and wedged the back under the doorknob.

It was exactly what he should have done the moment he arrived in the room. But instead, he'd been too caught up in Shelly and what was happening in her damnable fantasy.

"They're chocolate," Winona added, "not those old hard mints. Special ordered them myself right off the internet. They've got our name on the package and everything."

"Thanks, but no thanks. Have a good night," he added, trying to be polite despite the fact that she was wearing on his last nerve.

She didn't budge and he could feel her curiosity swirling into a frenzy, urging her to whip out the key in her pocket and let herself in anyway. Just to see what her newest guest was up to.

She didn't, but Colton knew it was just a matter of time. Cody had been right. He didn't belong in a motel room. He should have accepted his brother's offer and camped out at his place.

But it was hard seeing them now, remembering the past, the camaraderie they'd shared. The closeness.

Things could never be the same between them. They were different now. *He* was different.

Thanks to Rose.

She'd taken everything from him, and he'd let her. By not seeing her true nature. By not moving faster and getting home sooner. By not seeing the truth.

The treachery.

Never again.

He grabbed a nearby lamp and balanced it on the chair. If Winona tried anything, the lamp would fall and the noise would wake him up. It wasn't the high-powered security system Cody had protecting his spread, but it would have to do.

"Good night," he added.

Another indecisive moment and the old woman blew out an exasperated breath. "Same to you." Footsteps shuffled along the walkway, the sound fading as she made her way back to the office.

Colton damned himself yet again for getting caught off guard. For being antsy and unsettled and frustrated.

Thanks to Shelly.

He downed the last of the blood and shoved the empty plastic into the bottom of his bag. Dropping into a nearby chair, he powered up his computer and spent the next few hours re-reading the articles he'd downloaded about Holbrook's previous escapes.

He didn't learn anything new, but he did manage to kill some time and distract himself until exhaustion closed in and he fell into a deep, consuming sleep.

At least for a little while.

Until the sun came up and the hotel's owner started beating on his door again.

"It's motel policy," the old woman called out. "Everybody gets clean sheets along with a coupon for a complimentary piece of pie from the diner. Best pie you ever had, too."

"I'll pass on the pie," Colton managed to call out, despite the exhaustion tugging him under. "I had a late night. I really need to sleep."

"No problem, sugar. You get some shut-eye."

Thankfully.

"I'll be back in ten."

Forget biting the dust in the coming battle.

At the rate things were going, the old motel owner was sure to aggravate him to death long before he faced off with Rose.

7

"THIS AIN'T EVEN WARM." Beauford Truitt opened the white bakery box that Shelly sat next to the coffee-maker and peered inside. "They're all glazed," he declared, a scowl on his face.

"That's all that was left." Shelly stuffed her purse in her desk and did her damndest not to glance at the clock.

She already knew what time it was. It was two hours past her usual arrival time.

Two hours.

Late.

The truth stirred a memory of a small girl walking into her first grade class long after the bell had rang because her mother had slept in yet again.

It was an incident that had happened time and time again right after her Grandma Jean had passed away. Until Shelly had figured out how to set her own alarm and get herself off in the mornings.

She'd never been late since.

Until now.

Until him.

It had taken her forever to fall asleep after last night's Grade A fantasy, but once she'd managed to close her eyes, that had been it. Not even a full blown alarm or a bedroom full of bright morning sunlight had been enough to wake her.

No, it had taken ten phone calls from Bobby to finally drag her into the office.

"Are you okay?" he asked, coming up next to her.

"I'm fine." She hit the On button and powered up her computer, desperate to ignore the dark, sexy image that rushed at her and brought a burst of heat to her cheeks. Her nipples tingled and her thighs ached and she damned herself for being so weak.

"You don't look fine."

"Well, I am fine."

"You look different—"

"Did you finish the shift report?" she interrupted, desperate to change the subject and stifle the nagging voice that told her he was right.

She *was* different.

Forget calm and controlled and focused.

Her mind raced and her nerves buzzed and awareness rippled up and down her spine.

Sugar and caffeine, she reminded herself. She was hyped thanks to the two donuts and the extra large energy drink she'd had on the way over. The drink had been to wake her up while the glazed duo had been more of a desperate attempt to satisfy the craving that still ate away inside of her. A craving that had nothing to do with food and everything to do with the cowboy who'd kissed her senseless last night.

"I can't put my finger on it, but something's up with you," Bobby declared, his voice yanking her away from the detour her thoughts were about to take, straight into the land of the sexually deprived.

"Don't be silly." She sank down at her desk and opened her e-mail. "I look the way I always do." A quick look through Matt's e-mail verified that Colton had been telling the truth. He was a security specialist from county.

And he was coming back in exactly eight hours and fifty-two minutes and—

Bobby sank down on the corner of her desk, effectively killing her view of the clock. Thankfully.

"What?" she asked when his gaze narrowed.

"Are you wearing lipstick?"

Pale pink shimmer.

She'd bought the tube during a weak moment in Austin last year and stashed it in her dresser along with all of the other cosmetics she would never wear.

But you're wearing it right now, her conscience reminded her. *Right here. Right now. In front of everyone.*

"It's just lip balm," she blurted, pushing to her feet. "My lips were dry." *And tingling from the best kiss of my life. I needed something—anything—to kill the sensation.*

She certainly hadn't swiped it on in a last-ditch effort to look good for *him*.

"Have a donut." She snatched up the box and held it out to him. "I brought two dozen."

"There ain't no bear claws in there," Truitt reminded Bobby. "No long johns. Not even a dang fritter. And all because of Sleeping Beauty there."

"For the last time—I didn't sleep in. I had a broken water pipe."

"In-wall?" Bobby arched an eyebrow as he took a donut. "'Cause my brother-in-law is a really good sheetrock guy. I could give him a call—"

"External," she said. "My sheetrock's fine and I fixed the pipe myself." She whirled and made a beeline for the containment area before Bobby decided to chime in with more questions.

"Hey, where are you going with my donuts?" Truitt called after her.

"They're *my* donuts and I'm going to feed *my* prisoners."

She punched in the combination for the door leading to the back area. The lock clicked and the steel opened, and she left Bobby and Ranger Truitt staring after her.

She walked down the single hallway, the two cells situated on either side, facing each other. To the right, Honey sat flipping channels on the small TV Bobby had set up for her. To the left, Jimmy Holbrook lay stretched out on his bunk, a pair of headphones stuffed into his ears, the cord attached to a small transistor radio Beauford Truitt had allowed him to have. The Ranger's empty chair sat outside the doorway surrounded by a mountain of empty foam cups. The smell of coffee filled the air.

Shelly unearthed two donuts with a napkin and held them out to Honey. "I know the diner sent in breakfast this morning, but I thought you might want a snack."

The woman shook her head, her hair wild and unkempt, as if she'd spent the night tossing and turning. "Thanks, but no thanks. I don't do donuts. Too many calories." She pulled her knees up to her chest and Shelly felt a pang of guilt. Honey looked so tired. So worried. "Tell me again why I'm still sitting in here."

"Judge Myers is fishing in Port Aransas and decided to stay an extra day. He called this morning. He won't be back until tomorrow."

Misery washed over Honey's expression and guilt swirled through Shelly. "I'm so sorry about this. I'd let you out in a heartbeat if I could, but I have to follow procedure." Particularly with Beauford Truitt watching her every move. The man had already raised a fuss about the TV. "Matt's depending on me to run things by the book."

The woman pushed to her feet and paced the length of the cot. "But I've got orders to fill. And I promised Roy McGee I'd do a life-size steer made entirely of cupcakes for the chili cook-off finals on Saturday." She met Shelly's stare. "Daylight's burning and I'm falling more and more behind." Her gaze narrowed as if she'd just noticed something. "Are you wearing lipstick?"

"It's lip balm. My lips are getting chapped. Look, I know this is a pain," she continued, "but you just have to sit tight one more day. In the meantime, I'll drive out and talk to Walt." Walt Hornsby was the owner of the Sac-n-Pac who'd filed the complaint. "Maybe I can convince him to drop the charges."

"And maybe pigs will fly." The blonde shook her head. "He leases the building from Pinkie and her husband, which means he's stuck doing her dirty work and I'm stuck in here." She sank down on the mattress.

"Can I have one of those?"

The deep voice came from behind her and Shelly turned to see Jimmy Holbrook sitting on the edge of his bunk. He pulled the headset from around his neck and pushed to his feet.

He'd peeled off his shirt and wore only a pair of orange pants and a white wife-beater. He had the hard, muscular body of a lot of prisoners who had nothing better to do than spend their days lifting weights out in the yard. A large dragon tattoo covered one arm and crept up his neck, blowing fire around his Adam's apple. His dark hair was cut in a short military style. He looked tough. Dangerous. But there was something oddly disarming when he smiled. His steel blue eyes crinkled at the corners. Dimples cut into his stubbled cheeks and the menacing air that surrounded him seemed to ease.

It was no doubt the very reason he'd waltzed out of four prisons in as many years.

"Help yourself." Shelly held up the bakery box while he extended an arm through the bars and took one of the donuts.

Her gaze met his and a sense of déjà vu washed over her. Her stomach hollowed out and her lips tingled.

"Thanks." He ate half the donut in one bite before turning and walking back over to his bunk.

"Cute, ain't he?" Honey's voice drew Shelly around to find the woman standing at her cell door.

"He's a dangerous criminal."

"With one hell of a body." Honey stared past her and Shelly turned in time to see Jimmy down the rest of his donut and reach for his headset. He stuffed the buds back into his ears, positioned the radio on the bed and dropped to the floor for some push-ups. Muscles flexed and rippled and…okay, so he did have one hell of a body.

"He did push-ups all night." Honey's voice slid into her ears. "And sit-ups. And even some pull-ups on the overhead bar running across the door."

That explained Honey's haggard expression.

Shelly and Honey watched as he pushed up, then down. Up. Then down.

"Maybe I will have one of those donuts," Honey murmured. "Or two. I have a feeling it's going to be a long day."

Shelly glanced at her watch for the countless time, noting that she still had eight hours and forty-one minutes. "Tell me about it.

8

COLTON STOOD IN the shadows several hours after sunset and watched Shelly's car pull out of the parking lot. He'd parked his truck the next street over about an hour ago and had been waiting for her to leave ever since.

Bingo.

He stiffened against a nudge of disappointment and gathered his resolve. Walking into the Sheriff's office last night had taught him one important lesson—Shelly Lancaster was immune to his vamp charisma which meant it would be better, easier, to do what he had to do without her looking over his shoulder.

Kissing her had taught him an even bigger lesson. Shelly Lancaster was more than a distraction. She was downright dangerous. Instead of focusing on the upcoming battle with Rose, he'd spent the day tossing and turning and thinking about Shelly.

About how much he wanted her. And how much he needed her.

Like hell.

The only thing he needed was to avenge his family and silence the demons that haunted him once and for all. It's all he'd thought about since he was turned.

Revenge.

That should be the only thing on his mind, which was why he had every intention of keeping his distance. While he'd connected with her last night, they'd still only shared a kiss. Which meant that the thread that ran between them was fragile at best. It would fade and Colton meant to do everything in his power to speed up the process.

Namely he was staying far, far away from her.

His mind made up, he watched as her tail lights faded and then he started across the street.

The sharp scent of stale caffeine, old meatloaf and Liquid Paper hit him when he pushed open the door and stepped into the office. It was a one room set up with three desks situated here and there behind a large counter that served as the dispatch center. Jason Aldean drifted from a small CD player next to the radio.

Colton's gaze swept the area, drinking in the two most important details—the older gentleman with snow white hair and a pissed off expression who stood near the microwave and the younger man with a blond crew cut who sat hunkered over a pile of paperwork. The blond guy wore a Skull Creek Deputy's uniform, a badge pinned to his chest. He glanced up and his gaze locked with Colton's.

His name was John Cummins. He'd been with the Sheriff's office two years now. Married. Twins on the way. He'd just started his shift and already he was neck deep finishing up Bobby's paperwork because the rookie had been called out to County Road 21 to round up some kids rumored to be throwing cow patties at passing cars.

John paused, pen in hand. "What can I do you for?"

"The name's Colton Braddock." Colton held up the clearance packet Brent had dropped by the motel just after sunset, complete with a badge and ID card. "I'm doing the security upgrade."

Recognition dawned and John nodded. "Shelly said you'd be stopping by. 'Course, we all damn near gave up on you." He glanced at his watch. "It's awful late."

"Better late than never." Colton did another visual comb-over of the room, drinking in the last few details. Four large filing cabinets spread out against the far wall along with a small sidebar bearing a coffeemaker and microwave, as well as five reams of computer paper stacked in the corner.

"What exactly are you planning to do?" John asked, drawing Colton's attention.

"Nothing invasive tonight. Just a walk-through to assess the level of security."

"That ought to take about five seconds." The comment came from the old man. He held a meat loaf sandwich in one hand and a napkin in the other. Swiping at a ketchup smudge near the corner of his mouth, he eyeballed Colton. "Let me tell you, this place is a joke when it comes to security. That's why me and old blue, here—" He tapped the gun at his hip. "—are keeping a close eye on everything."

"This here's Ranger Truitt." John waved a hand toward the old man. "He's helping us out while Holbrook's in-house."

"What he means is I'm doing all the work." The Ranger took another bite.

"I'm sure the folks in town appreciate your support." Colton stared deep into the Ranger's eyes and willed him to listen. *Obey.* "I bet you're tired. Maybe it's time for you to sit down and take a load off." He motioned to a nearby chair. *Now.*

The man looked ready to argue as he swallowed his mouthful, but then his jaw went slack. A glazed look came over his face and his head bobbed in agreement. He stumbled backward a few steps and sank down into the nearby chair, the sandwich in his hands forgotten, his eyes vacant, his mind seemingly a million miles away.

"What the hell?" That's what John was thinking just as Colton turned back to the Deputy.

"You look tired, too, Deputy Cummins," Colton added, killing the man's thoughts before he could speculate any further. "Very tired. I think now might be a good time for you to get a little shut-eye, as well." *Sleep.* He concentrated all of his energy into the silent command and sent it spiraling across the room.

In a matter of seconds, John's expression went from alarmed to passive. He leaned forward and slumped over his desk. His eyes closed and a heart-beat later, a steady snore filled the room.

Colton didn't waste any time. He made a bee-line for the door leading to the containment area and punched in the code Brent had given him. The door powered open and in a matter of seconds, he was standing in the hallway that ran between the two cells.

Ranger Truitt's empty chair sat at the very end of the hallway, surrounded by a litter of coffee-stained foam cups. Colton's gaze swiveled past the right-sided cell and zeroed in on the male to his left.

Jimmy Holbrook lay sideways on his bunk, fac-ing the wall. A blanket covered his lower half. His soft, steady snores filled the air.

"Sssshhhh." The female voice sounded behind him and he half turned to see a tall, leggy blonde standing at the bars.

Her name was Honey Gentry and she'd been wrongfully accused of trespassing thanks to a jeal-ous old woman who suspected her of cheating with her husband. But Honey had given up cavorting with half the town's married men to pursue her true pas-sion—baking cupcakes. Only she was stuck here when she should have been working on her biggest order to date and she was damned frustrated about it. And she'd been celibate for over six months on account of she'd joined Sexoholics Anonymous and it was part of her twelve steps.

Her hair was mussed, her mascara smudged due to a stressful, sleepless night courtesy of the hottie across from her. Her hands trembled ever so slightly as she grabbed the bars and anxiety knotted her muscles. He could practically hear the energy bubbling inside her as she pressed a finger to her lips, signaling him to keep quiet.

His gaze locked with hers and, sure enough, he read the anxiety she was feeling. It swirled with a volatile mixture of frustration and hunger that gave her a wired look.

He could definitely relate. His own muscles felt tight and bunched. His fingers still tingled from the feel of Shelly's soft skin. His stomach hollowed out and his gut twisted.

"He just fell asleep. *Finally*," she whispered. "I'll lose my friggin' mind *and* my figure if you wake him up again." When Colton arched an eyebrow, she added. "He exercises. A lot." She'd never been into bad boys, but seeing all those muscles move and bulge had given her a new appreciation for the dark and dangerous. "If I have to watch him even one more minute...." She swallowed. Hard. "I'll dive back into that box over there." She motioned to the white bakery container sitting on her bunk. "And it won't be pretty."

"I won't wake him," he promised. "If you do something for me."

Desperate blue eyes held his. "Anything."

"Sleep." He held her gaze long enough to send her the few steps back toward the bunk. She sank down and her eyes closed.

And then it was time to move.

Colton pulled a small spray bottle from his pocket. Liquid silver. Cody's friends and fellow vampires at Skull Creek Choppers—the town's legendary custom motorcycle shop—had cooked up the concoction by mixing molten silver with a specially formulated quick-drying paint. The color matched the bars and would blend in evenly once sprayed on.

Colton shook the container for a few seconds the way Brent had told him to, then flicked the nozzle and activated the spraying mechanism. Leaning up, he started in a sweeping motion at the top of Holbrook's cell door and worked his way down.

Forget the age-old myths regarding vampire repellants. Garlic, holy water and crosses didn't stand a chance against a true vampire. Sunlight and wooden stakes posed the only real threats. But silver did pack a powerful punch if used properly. While the metal wouldn't kill on contact, it did burn like a sonofabitch. More than enough to stop Rose and keep her from releasing Jimmy a fifth time.

And then Colton himself would stop her for good.

He finished up with the paint and closed the lid. A drop of paint hit his skin. White hot pain shot through him. He ground his teeth against the sensation until the heat fizzled into a steady throb and he could actually see again. He damned himself for not being more careful and stared down at the raw, smoking flesh. Despite the three bags of blood he'd had back at the motel, the wound wasn't healing.

It wouldn't, not unless he helped it along.

An image of Shelly pushed into his brain, her body slick and wet from the tub, her sweet heat tantalizing against his tongue, her energy so potent and mesmerizing that he couldn't get enough.

But that hadn't been real. Rather, he'd been caught up in her fantasy, seeing and feeling her, but not truly participating. He was still weak. Hungry.

For any woman, he reminded himself.

For one woman.

His gaze shifted to Honey who sat on the bunk, eyes closed, a half smile on her face as if she were dreaming the most pleasant of dreams. His hand screamed and his gut twisted.

"Come."

The command whispered through his head, pushed from his thoughts, and she looked up. Her gaze met his. Her breath quickened in anticipation. She'd been so worked up all day and nothing, not even the sugary donuts had been enough to curb her appetite. But he could. He could give her what she wanted, and take what he desperately needed, satisfying them both.

A few steps and she met him at the cell door. She

really was an attractive female with her long hair and curvaceous figure, and she didn't seem the least bit anxious to hide any of it. She wore shorts and a fitted top that left little to the imagination unlike one infuriating Deputy who made it a point to cover everything up and make him wonder what lay beneath.

After last night, he knew.

He nixed the thought and watched as Honey extended a French-manicured hand through the bars. She held out one delicate wrist.

At the moment of contact, he felt the first bubble of energy. It slipped into his fingertips and crested through his body. But the sensation was weak. Fleeting. She wasn't nearly as warm as he'd expected. As luscious. As stirring.

She wasn't Shelly.

He drop-kicked the ridiculous notion and tamped down on the sudden regret that rushed through him.

"Stay away from Holbrook," he murmured as he stared deep into her eyes. "He's dangerous and you can do a hell of a lot better."

And then he dropped her hand, broke the spell and walked away.

Not because of Shelly, mind you.

No, he had more important matters propelling him away from Honey Gentry than simple infuriating lust over one stubborn Deputy.

He powered open the door and locked it behind him. He'd already pushed his luck with the two men out front. They were under his spell, but it wouldn't last long. Honey was a different story. Females were more susceptible to male vampires and vice versa. She would stay out of it for at least a few hours, the spell fading gradually as the distance between them grew. But the other two?

His gaze shifted from the Deputy who slumped over his desk, to the Texas Ranger sitting stone-faced in a nearby chair. They were still mindless, but there was no guarantee how long that would last. They could wake up any second and start asking questions about the void in their memory. Then Colton would be back to square one, mesmerizing them all over again, wasting more precious time when he needed to get back to his truck and get on with his surveillance.

Just in case Rose showed up early.

He ignored the nagging voice that told him she wasn't anywhere close. That his brothers were right and he was wasting time when he could be resting and gathering his strength instead of waiting. Watching.

Fantasizing.

He left the jail and rounded the building, heading for the back fence that edged the parking lot.

Fantasizing? Hardly.

He was doing no such thing when it came to Shelly Lancaster. And he certainly wasn't running away like a bat out of hell because of her. Because she'd gotten under his skin and the thought of touching another woman had bothered him a helluva lot more than he'd expected. Because he could still smell

Shelly's sweet scent and taste her ripe essence and hear the steady staccato of her heartbeat and—

"What the hell are you doing here?" Her voice echoed and he whirled to find her standing in the parking lot behind him, her keys in one hand, a Red Bull in the other.

She couldn't have looked more different from the bombshell locked up in cell number two. While she'd changed out of her drab uniform, she'd opted for an even more drab pair of gray sweatpants and a matching Texas A & M sweatshirt, the monstrous sleeves pushed up to her elbows. Instead of long and flowing and sexy, her hair was pulled back into a tight ponytail and there wasn't a trace of makeup on her face. No lipstick plumping her lips, inviting his kiss. No shadow accenting her eyes and luring him closer. Nothing.

And damned if she still wasn't the most beautiful woman he'd ever seen.

Instantly, his gut twisted and his chest hitched and he finally admitted to himself that his damned frustration had nothing to do with the need for a real flesh and blood woman and everything to do with *her*.

Because she was the most sexually frustrated woman he'd ever come into contact with. It was her energy that drew him. Distracted him.

And it had to stop now, before it got any worse.

At the rate he was going, Rose would show up and he would be too wired to even notice.

"It's almost ten o'clock." Her gaze narrowed. "Since when is it standard operating procedure to do a security evaluation at this hour?" Without waiting for his reply, she continued, "You should have been here hours ago. I waited an entire day—*all* day," she said accusingly. "I even rearranged my schedule so I'd be free to show you around. I sent Bobby to chase down six of Mr. McGee's cows all by himself because I was sticking around here, waiting for you—"

"We should have sex," he murmured, cutting her off mid-sentence.

Her jaw snapped shut and her head snapped up. Surprise glittered hot and bright in her eyes. Her breath caught and she stared at him for a long, tense moment, trying to comprehend his words. And failing. "What did you just say?" she finally asked.

He stepped closer. "You." Another step. "Me." Step. Step. *"Sex."* And then he kissed her.

9

IT WASN'T THE BEST pick-up line Shelly had ever heard.

There was no smooth analogy. No flirtatious play on words. No seductive wink to punctuate the end of the sentence.

At the same time, it was the only pick-up line— with the exception of "Wanna play hide the summer sausage?" courtesy of Billy Rankin back in the ninth grade—that had ever been directed straight at her. And for some reason that all-important fact packed an awful powerful punch.

Colton Braddock wanted to have sex with her. *He* wanted to have sex with *her*.

The truth echoed in her head for one triumphant moment before realization dawned and she remembered that there was no way she could allow herself to go through with this. They were business colleagues, and Shelly never mixed with business with pleasure. She had an image to protect. She needed the confidence of every citizen in town when election time rolled around which was why she'd called the few men desperate enough to believe the ad and set them straight first thing that morning.

But Colton Braddock wasn't an impressionable voter. He was simply passing through. Temporary. So what if she let her image slip just a little? He was in town for a few days at the most and suddenly there seemed nothing wrong with getting up close and personal.

As long as they set down a few ground rules first.

She stiffened, gathered her strength and pulled away from the best kiss of her life.

She stared up at him and for a few frantic heartbeats, she actually forgot her first rule. He looked so tall, dark and delicious in a black T-shirt and worn, faded Wranglers, the hems frayed around his scuffed boots. He'd left his hat behind and there was nothing except a thick fringe of black lashes shadowing his pale, translucent gaze that swept from her head to her toes and back up again.

In a flash, she had the insane thought that she never, ever wanted to be with any other man. It was him. It would always be him.

Not.

This wasn't about forever. It was about now.

Right now.

"Okay." The word was out before she could stop it.

He seemed surprised for a split-second, before his expression faded into sheer determination. "Let's go—"

"One night," she added, eager to make sure they were on the same page. "And then it's over. You go your way and I'll go mine. And you keep your mouth shut about the whole thing."

His lips drew into a tight line and a muscle ticked in his jaw, as if he meant to argue. That, or kiss her senseless again. His eyes darkened and smoldered. She felt his strong hands at her waist, ready to pull her closer. Electricity zipped up her spine.

The moment held for several fast, furious heart-beats, but then the tension seemed to ease and he nodded.

"Tonight and nothing more."

"*And* you keep your mouth shut. I'm running for Sheriff in six months and I won't do anything that might jeopardize that. I've been working for this my entire life."

A sexy grin tugged at his lips and a gleam danced in his eyes. "Darlin', I never kiss and tell."

His deep voice confirmed what she'd already suspected and a sliver of warmth went through her. Colton Braddock was a lot more likeable than she cared to admit.

"What else?" He arched an eyebrow.

"I need to check in and tie up a few things in the office first." The grin faded and he looked as if he wanted to argue. Fat chance. Shelly had her mind made up. If they were doing this, it was going to be by her rules. "Meet me in an hour. My place."

Surprisingly enough, he didn't protest. Instead, he

dipped his head for one last kiss to seal the agreement, and then he all but disappeared right before her eyes.

A strange sense of *uh-oh* wiggled through her as she stared at the empty spot where he'd stood only moments before, but then anticipation got the best of her. She became acutely aware of her sweat suit and old sneakers and… Yikes.

She turned and hurried around to the front of the building where she'd left her car. She had one hour to pull off the makeover of a lifetime and the clock was already ticking.

She'd lied to Colton.

Forget loose ends at the office. She'd needed time to trade her sweats and sensible cotton briefs for *this*.

She stared at the drawer full of lingerie, everything from leopard print bras to black sequined thongs. Practically the entire on-line catalog at Naughty Nights. Her very own hidden treasure of indulgence. Perfect for the rendezvous of a lifetime.

She reached for hot pink lace bra and matching thong. A few seconds later, she dabbed on lipstick and a little mascara, and then surveyed the results in the mirror.

For a split-second, time sucked her back and she remembered standing in the doorway, watching her mother get ready for an evening out, praying all the while that she would change her mind and stay home.

Just this once.

She shook away the image and tamped down the urge to peel off the trashy underwear. Unlike her mother, she didn't have any kids to take care of. Even more, she could control herself. One encounter, and then the sexy nothings went back in the drawer where they belonged and Colton Braddock moved on to the next town.

But while she had plenty of lingerie, sexy clothes were a different matter. She turned toward her closet and frowned.

Rifling through a sea of beige cotton, she unearthed her one and only dress—a strappy, summer number that she'd bought during a training seminar in Austin. The dress was white silk with pale yellow flowers and a fringe of yellow lace at the neckline. The tags were still intact, proof that the dress had been more of an impulse buy than anything she would actually wear in her normal life.

But tonight wasn't the norm.

She tugged the tags loose and was just undoing the side zipper when the doorbell rang.

What the…?

Her gaze ping-ponged to the clock. Reality zapped her and she realized that she'd spent an entire half hour angsting over undies.

She stepped into the dress and shimmied and wiggled until she managed to get it up and over her hips. Okay, so trying the dress on when she'd bought it might have been a good idea. But she'd been in a hurry and desperate to do it on the fly while Bobby finished up his lunch at a nearby pub. She'd grabbed it and paid for it and the deed had been done.

Shoving her arms into the straps, she drew a deep breath and pulled the bodice up and over her chest. Frantic fingers plucked at the side zipper, pulling and tugging until she managed to get it up and over her hips. She sucked in a breath to bring it the rest of the way home, but it didn't help. The zipper wouldn't budge past her waist.

The doorbell rang again, sending a message of *hurry the hell up* through her. She fought with the zipper a few more seconds, but it was no use. The dress was a lost cause. She pushed the zipper the opposite way, ready to shed the dress and opt for her sweats, but the metal teeth were stuck. She pushed and tugged, but it refused to budge—

Rrrrrrrriiiiinnnnngggggg!

The doorbell sounded again and she glanced out the upstairs window in time to see Colton Braddock step down off her front porch.

She had the fleeting thought that he might be leaving. Giving up. *No!*

She snapped up her sweatshirt and pulled it down over her head and chest so that it made the sundress look like a skirt. Hurrying down the stairs, she threw open the door. The porch light cast a soft yellow glow that pushed back the shadows and bathed her empty doorstep.

She stepped out onto the porch and scanned the surrounding area, seeing the tiny postage stamp-size yard that she loved so much, the flower bushes lining the perimeter. The familiar black pick-up still sat in the driveway behind her car and relief swamped her.

"I was starting to think you'd changed your mind." His deep voice rumbled in her ear a split second before she felt his presence directly behind her.

"I was getting dressed." She whirled and found herself face to face with Colton Braddock.

He arched one dark brow as his gaze dropped to the sweatshirt. "Weren't you wearing that earlier?"

"Technically, yes. It's a long story. One you'd rather not hear. Trust me."

A grin tugged at his lips and her breath caught. Her gaze collided with his and her heart gave a double thump. He had the most incredible eyes that looked almost silver in the dim light. So hot and liquid and mesmerizing.

She felt herself being pulled into the warm depths. It would be so easy to lose herself. To dive head first and forget about everyone and everything. To strip naked despite the fact that she was standing smack dab on her front porch. Anyone could walk by. Mrs. Fleming from next door could be watering her tulips or Mr. Sandowski could be out walking his dog. Yet staring deep into his eyes, she didn't care. It was about doing this with him, right now, right here, *right now,* regardless of the consequences.

She reached for the hem of her sweatshirt and an image rushed at her, of her mother stumbling in after a late night, tearing at her clothes as she fought to get closer to the man with her. She'd been mindless of her two little girls sitting on the sofa, waiting for her. She'd been a slave to the same desperation that suddenly gripped Shelly.

Her hand stalled and she fought for control. "Not now," she said, her hand trembling. "Not here."

He started to protest, but she pressed a finger to his lips. The feel of his mouth sent a burst of need through her and her body vibrated from the force. She grabbed his hand and led him toward the door. He stalled just shy of the threshold and she glanced back at him.

"Say it," he growled.

"Say what?"

"Ask me to come in."

She nodded, but he didn't budge. She was struck again with the odd thought that something wasn't quite right.

That he wasn't quite right.

But then he leaned forward and kissed her, hard and brutal, and she forgot everything except the heat singing through her body.

"Say it," he murmured again against her lips.

"Come inside," she heard herself say. "Please."

He followed her in. The door slammed shut behind them and she whirled to face him. Her breaths came fast and quick as she grasped the sweatshirt and pulled it up and over her head. Cotton hit the ground at her feet. The cool rush of air from the overhead vent teased her nipples through the lace of her bra and excitement chased up her spine.

"Here," she breathed. "Now." She stepped toward him.

10

HE WANTED TO KISS her again.

The truth struck as Colton stood in the foyer and watched her work at the clasp on the bra. It hit the ground on top of the sweatshirt and his undead heart stopped beating.

Yes, he wanted to kiss her again. But it went beyond the need gripping his entire body. There was something deep inside of him, something urgent and fierce and possessive, that roared to life and propelled him forward. To brand her as his. Now and forever.

No!

He fought the crazy feeling and bypassed her luscious lips. His mouth went to one ripe nipple.

He hauled her close and bent her backward as he feasted on the hard tip, laving and sucking, but it wasn't enough. His teeth grazed her tender flesh and his incisors tingled. Desire pounded through him, fierce and demanding and *different*. The truth resonated through him as he fought to keep from sinking his fangs deep and tasting her sweet essence.

Because *she* was different.

The thought twisted at him as he scooped her up into his arms and turned toward the living room to his right.

Near the large leather sofa, he eased her to her feet, sliding her down the length of his body in a move that made them both gasp. She was so soft and warm and his body trembled.

Their gazes locked as he reached out and touched the zipper of the sundress caught at her waist. His heart pounded and his pulse raced and an ache gripped him from the inside out. He tugged and the zipper gave way. The teeth parted.

She grasped the material and shoved it down as fast as possible. She'd been waiting for this far too long and she didn't want to give herself the chance to change her mind. Even more, she didn't want to give *him* the chance to change *his* mind.

He read the thought before it faded into the heat of her gaze and suddenly he wasn't half as anxious to satisfy his own hunger as he was to slow down and satisfy hers. To prove to her that she didn't need a skimpy dress or barely there underwear to be desirable to a man.

To him.

"Sexy isn't about the package, darlin'," he murmured. "It's a state of mind."

She looked surprised and startled that he was so tuned into her thoughts.

But then the expression faded into a rush of insecurity. "Nice packaging doesn't hurt."

Not that she would know. She'd never wrapped herself up to please a man before. No fancy underwear or frilly dresses. She had an image to protect and she wasn't about to destroy it by giving in to some silly need to play the soft, tempting female.

It was all about being strong. In control.

"There's nothing wrong with letting go once in a while." He dropped his gaze in a slow, deliberate trek down the length of her body before following the same path back up, from her calves to her lush thighs, the strip of lace barely concealing the heart of her. "You *are* a soft, tempting female, Shelly, no matter how much that pisses you off at times."

"It doesn't piss me off." At least it wasn't pissing her off at the moment. No, right now she wanted to sink down to the couch, part her legs and let him inside.

"Do it," he murmured. "Don't deny yourself. Let go. Just this once." He touched her, circling her ripe nipple and she gasped.

Surprise followed by heated satisfaction slid through her and the worried pinch between her eyebrows eased. While he couldn't see every thought because her stubbornness kept shutting the door, he could read her features. The bright flare of her brilliant eyes. The goose bumps that danced up her arms. The pink flush that crept up her neck. The need.

He swallowed, his throat suddenly dry. With a sweep of his tongue, he licked his lips. The urge to feel her pressed against his mouth nearly sent him over the edge. He wanted to part her with his tongue and unleash everything she fought so desperately to keep bottled up. Desire pounded, steady, demanding, and sent the blood jolting through his veins at an alarming rate.

He urged her back onto the couch and surprisingly, she let him. He dropped to his knees between her legs, his shoulders wedging her further apart. His fingertips circled the rose-colored nipple, and he inhaled sharply when the already turgid peak ripened even more.

Leaning over her, he touched his lips to her navel, dipped his tongue inside and swirled. She whimpered, the sound urging him on. He licked a path up her fragrant skin, teasing and nibbling, until he reached one full breast. Closing his lips over her swollen nipple, he pulled and tugged.

He swept his hands downward, over her flat, quivering belly, to her panties. He dipped a hand beneath the lace and traced the slit between her legs. She gasped when he parted her. He pushed one finger deliciously deep. Heat surrounded him, sucking him in and sending a jolt of hunger through him that shook him to his very core.

She trembled and gasped and, just like that, she

came apart. His hand started to tingle as he drank in the sweet, bubbling energy of her climax. The sensation spread through him, pulsing up his arm, into his shoulder, his chest, pushing out the cold and filling him with a hot, vibrating burst of sensation.

He closed his eyes and drank in the feeling, relishing it for a long, delicious moment. Forget plunging his cock deep inside of her. This alone was ecstasy for him. For any vampire.

More than enough.

It was all about a woman's orgasm. About soaking up *her* energy, not spending his own.

"If I didn't know better, I'd say you're enjoying this more than me." The sound of her voice slipped into his thoughts and he opened his eyes to find her staring up at him.

"I'd be a fool not to. You're something else."

He said it with such sincerity that Shelly almost believed him. But this was the heat of the moment and a rock hard erection could impair the sharpest man's thinking. "You don't have to sweet talk me into bed. I'm practically there. Speaking of which, shouldn't we head upstairs?"

His grin was slow and sinful and oh, so delicious. He lowered his head and drew the throbbing tip of one breast into the moist heat of his mouth, and suddenly the only thing on her mind was touching him. She slid her hands over his shoulders, feeling his warm skin and hard muscle through the soft cotton of his T-shirt.

He suckled her, his teeth grazing the soft globe of flesh, nipping and biting the turgid nipple with just enough pressure to make her gasp. Her breast swelled and throbbed.

When he licked a path across her skin to coax the other breast in the same torturous manner, a decadent heat spiraled through her and she moved her pelvis. She wanted him surrounding her, inside of her.

"Easy, sugar," he said as if he read the desperation. "We've got all night."

But Shelly didn't want all night. All night meant a morning after. As in waking up with each other and sharing an awkward goodbye in the bright light of day.

And while she'd never been the one saying goodbye, she'd witnessed it too many times to count.

Never again.

This was about indulging herself right now. About living out a brief, temporary fantasy that wouldn't haunt her in the days to come.

No, she didn't want all night. She wanted one really good climax with him inside of her and her falling apart in his arms. One. And then she could get past the frustration and set her mind on what really mattered—her job.

"I have to be at work early tomorrow." Desperate hands reached for him and he stiffened. "We should hurry up and get to the good stuff. Then you can go home and I'll get some sleep." *And then it'll be over.*

Her hands skimmed his shoulders and drew him closer, but he didn't budge.

"I don't think so." His voice pushed past the pounding of her pulse and she realized that something was wrong.

Her eyelids fluttered open in time to see him push to his feet and stumble backward.

He looked as surprised as she felt.

"What's wrong?"

But he didn't seem to know any more than she did. He glanced around as if desperate for a distraction. His gaze hooked on the bookshelf she'd inherited from her Grandma Jean, along with the dozens of romance novels boxed in the back of her closet.

Rows of how-to books lined the shelves now, everything from gun collecting to softball techniques. All in keeping with the image she'd fought so hard to build.

It was an image that was slipping away as she lay open and exposed to Colton Braddock.

"Please." Her voice was shameless. "Don't stop."

But he had to. She could see it in his expression and while he didn't look all that pleased about it, he shook his head anyway. "It's getting really late. I should go."

"But what about the bedroom?"

His gaze locked with hers for a split-second. "I guess we'll just have to make up for it tomorrow night."

"But that's not part of the deal—" she protested, but he was already heading for the door.

She caught a quick glimpse of his face, the determined set to his jaw, the fire blazing in his liquid eyes, before he disappeared. Hinges creaked. Wood slammed. And just like that, he disappeared and Shelly found herself left with nothing but her fantasies to keep her company.

Again.

11

THE PAST WASN'T just haunting him. It was driving him crazy.

One hundred percent certifiable.

That was the only explanation for what he'd just done. She'd been right there. Open and waiting. *Ready.*

"And then it'll be over."

Her voice echoed in his head and he slammed his foot down on the accelerator, speeding down the road, feeding the distance between them.

He hung a left at the edge of town and headed north, until the pavement turned to gravel and rocks spewed against the underside of the pick-up. The road narrowed, cutting a path between a stretch of rich, green pastureland. To his right, he glimpsed a rustic two-story white rock house in the far distance. He drove another fifty yards, following the instructions Cody had left on his cell, until he got a better view of the structure. A gate marked the entrance, but Colton didn't turn in. Instead, he pulled over onto the side of the road and killed the engine.

It was just half past midnight. Late for regular folks. Early for a vampire.

Lights beamed from the downstairs windows. A rustic Texas star light fixture gleamed near the front door, illuminating a wide front porch and a hand-carved cedar bench.

The house looked so familiar and for a brief moment, time sucked him back and he saw a newly whitewashed two-story house with red shutters and a wide wraparound porch. Curtains billowed at the windows and the scent of his momma's infamous cherry pie drifted from inside.

Home.

The Circle B had been in his family for two generations, passed down from his grandfather to his mother, an only child. She'd loved it and nurtured it more than any man, a helluva lot more than her no-good excuse for a husband did, a man who'd disappeared the first chance he'd had. The loss hadn't phased her. She'd had her home. One she was eager to pass on to the next in line when the time came.

First Colton.

Then his son.

The image of CJ with his bright blue eyes and dark hair faded into that of a woman with red hair and lying eyes. *Rose.*

He felt the familiar tightening in his chest and stiffened, focusing on the heat in his belly. The anger.

Vengeance.

That's why he was here.

Not because he missed his brothers, or because he wanted to make up for lost time. Or even because he desperately craved the peace and happiness they'd all managed to find even if they *were* vampires.

There was no peace for Colton. He'd failed his family. His son.

Because of Rose.

She would pay dearly for her treachery. He would make sure of it, even if it wouldn't come close to easing the guilt. The isolation. The loneliness.

The thought crept up on him so fast that he didn't have time to slam his mind against it.

Lonely?

Fire and damnation, he wasn't lonely. He was simply alone. He liked being alone. That's why he kept his distance from his ranch hands and left their supervision to his foreman. He didn't have to worry over them himself. Over getting too close or too attached. He didn't have to worry about letting anyone down.

Again.

He shook his head against the notion and focused on the bench sitting on Cody's porch. A cuddle bench. That's what his ma had called them way back when. They'd had one just like it sitting on their front porch back at the Circle B.

She'd caught Cody curled up on it more than once with some girl or another and so the name had stuck.

Not that Colton had ever tried it out for himself. He'd been too busy running cattle, desperate to pull his weight and support his new bride the way he'd promised Rose's daddy when the man had come calling with a shotgun and the news that his only daughter was pregnant. She'd named Colton as the father and the man had wanted a proper wedding.

But there'd been no need for that sawed off shotgun. Colton was more than ready to do his duty. Since his father had left at an early age, he'd been carrying the weight of responsibility for his family. Doing his duty was nothing new to him and so he'd done the right thing, determined to be the father he'd never had.

He'd never had the chance.

He slammed his foot down on the gas. Tires spewed gravel as he swerved back onto the road and drove a few miles until he saw the old farmhouse that had once been the only building on Cody's land. He pulled the truck over and killed the engine. While he wouldn't take Cody up on his offer to stay in the main house, he wouldn't mind bunking out here.

Colton was used to roughing it. When he was driving cattle, he slept in a cabin on the back forty of his property. A good sleeping bag and a few well-placed hay bales was all he needed to protect him from the sunlight.

Even better, this place was a good ten miles outside of town, far away from the motel and the nosey old woman making his days a living hell. And far, far away from Shelly and her damnable fantasies.

Boots hit the gravel as he climbed from behind the wheel and started for the old house. The paint had all but peeled off the brown shutters. The once white-washed walls were now gray and weathered. The porch steps were rotted and falling down. It was just a shell of what it had once been, far from the brand spanking new house Cody had built for his bride. Still, it held the same appeal. The same familiar layout that reminded Colton so much of home.

Unfortunately, it wasn't in good enough shape to provide adequate refuge for a vampire. He circled the house and started for the faded red barn that stood out back. While the house had a lot of roof damage thanks to past storms, the barn seemed to be made of tougher stuff. The metal roof was still sound, the structure weathered but sturdy.

Perfect.

The hinges creaked and groaned as he pulled the door open and walked inside. The musty smell of hay and leather and rotting wood filled his nostrils and he felt a pang of regret that his brother had traded this place for the shiny metal barn situated behind his new house.

This place had character, from the kids' names carved into one of the beams, to the old leather saddle still resting atop one of the stalls. A wall of antique tools lined the opposite side of the barn. A hand saw. A circular crank. Several notching tools. A wood stove for heating. He walked deeper inside and saw the work bench. His nostrils flared. His finally tuned senses picked up the faint trace of sawdust that had settled into the beams. Whoever had lived here had probably built the place and even hand-tooled that saddle.

He traced his hand over the leather and remembered the ancient bookcase in Shelly's living room with its scratches and worn edges. She was obviously the kind of woman who appreciated a nice antique, regardless of whether it was a bookshelf, or even a cuddle bench.

Not that he was going to make her one. The last thing he wanted was to cuddle with her, for Chrissake. Their relationship was all about sex. He knew it and so did she.

That was exactly why he'd walked out on her.

He had at least three days to kill and Shelly Lancaster was interested in just one night. All the more reason to slow things down a little. Otherwise he would have to find someone else to sate the hunger that ripped through him.

He wasn't doing that.

Shelly was too perfect. Too ripe. Too ready. Too repressed. She fed the need like no one else and so he meant to take his time. And draw things out for as long as possible.

He wanted Shelly. And he meant to have her.

At least until his past showed up and he said goodbye to everyone and everything.

12

"THANK GOD," Honey declared when Shelly walked into the cell area with another pastry box early the next morning.

Early as in nine-thirty.

Not only had she missed her alarm again, but she'd slept even later thanks to Colton Braddock and his announcement that he wanted to see her again.

Despite her very specific ground rules.

Excitement whispered through her, followed by a quick jolt of anxiety because the last thing, the very *last* thing she wanted was to spend another day like yesterday.

She'd been on pins and needles, waiting, wondering. Distracted. To the point that she'd been acting completely out of sorts.

"Are you wearing lipstick again?" Honey's question drew her from her mental tirade and confirmed the vicious truth.

"It's lip balm," she said, swiping at the Pink Passion with the back of her hand. "The drugstore only had the tinted stuff."

Honey swallowed her mouthful of donut. "Mind if I borrow some?"

"Be my guest." She watched as Honey slathered on Pink Passion, her gaze directed at the man sitting in the opposite cell. He was on his back on the floor, hands behind his head, ear buds stuffed into his ears, music turned up. He counted as he did a continuous rhythm of sit-ups. He'd shed his shirt and his abs flexed each time he folded up. Then down. Then up.

Oh, boy.

Shelly found herself wondering if Colton's abs were as defined. In her fantasies they were, but she'd yet to see for herself.

She wanted to.

She wanted it more than she wanted her next breath, and that scared her more than anything. She refused to get so caught up in a man that she forgot everything that really mattered.

The way her mother had.

No. She wasn't repeating that mistake. Ever.

"Thanks." Honey handed over the tube, but Shelly shook her head.

"Keep it."

"You've got good coloring." Honey slipped the tube into her pocket. "I bet you'd look good in a red lipstick."

"You know everything about make-up, don't you?"

"Been wearing it since I was thirteen. You should try a little eye shadow, too." Honey unearthed a donut from the box and took a big bite, savoring the mouthful for a long moment. "Fix yourself up a little and you might land yourself a boyfriend."

"Maybe I'm not looking for a boyfriend."

"Honey, we're all looking for a boyfriend. At the very least, we'd like somebody to keep things interesting every now and then."

Now would be good, Shelly thought to herself, her nerves still buzzing from last night. Very good.

"Is that how you do it?"

"Do what?"

"Get a guy? You fix yourself up."

"That, and I use a little technique I like to call the three B's." When Shelly arched an eyebrow, Honey added, "Boobs, butt and bending over. It's foolproof. See, you start with a really skimpy dress that's cut down to there." She motioned to her cleavage. "And up to here." She swept a hand to her upper thigh. "That way when you bend over, the dress hikes up just enough to give whoever is looking a sneak peak at your goodies. Then bam, they're following you home for as long as you want."

"And what if it doesn't work?"

Honey smiled. "It *always* works. See, men are visual. Give them plenty to look at and you'll have them eating out of the palm of your hand." She shoved the last of the donut into her mouth. "Just to cinch the deal though," she said in between chews, "I always have a red velvet cake on stand by."

"What if he doesn't like red velvet?"

"The cake isn't for him, sugar. It's for you. After you've wowed him with the dress, or lack of, you cut yourself a big piece of red velvet, or chocolate or carrot or whatever floats your boat, and eat it real nice and slow." She demonstrated with another donut, taking bite after bite, her movements so slow and deliberate and seductive, that Shelly felt her own stomach hollow out. Honey finished by sweeping her tongue along her bottom lip. "No way will he be able to watch that and not jump your bones."

If only.

Shelly made a mental note to pick up a red velvet cake on her way home. While she couldn't imagine that Colton Braddock would put her off another night, she wasn't taking any chances. She was pulling out all the stops and getting him into bed tonight. Then her anxiety would end and she could get back to her life. To being on time—to work and the effin' donut shop.

"No lemon crème?" Honey stared hopefully as she searched through what was left in the bakery box.

"I'm afraid not. They were all out by the time I got there."

"Oh, well." She shrugged and cast a hungry gaze at Holbrook. "It's not like I have to put up with Mr. Fitness over there for too much longer. I'll be out in less than an hour and then it's back to walking the straight and narrow with my cupcakes. Speaking of which, is Judge Meyers in yet?"

"About that." Shelly shook her head. "I know he was supposed to be in by nine, but when I came in Bobby said his secretary had postponed his morning cases."

"She *what?*"

"It seems he had a flat on his way back from Port A and won't be back until lunch."

"I can't sit here until lunch," Honey screeched. "I've got things to do. I've got deliveries coming by my place and cupcakes to bake and a celibacy vow that I'm this close to breaking thanks to him." She pointed at Jimmy. "You have to let me out of here."

"I wish I could. I really do." Particularly since the charges were bogus and Judge Meyers was sure to throw them out. "But Bobby booked you and that means you're in the system. I can't just let you walk without a court order." When Honey's face fell, she added, "But I can head out to your place and sign for the flour and sugar."

"You would do that for me?"

"You bet." Especially since it meant getting away from Bobby, who'd all but freaked when she'd walked in late again. *And* wearing lipstick. Seriously. It was lipstick, for heaven's sake. It's not like she looked that out of sorts. She *was* female.

Then again, that was the point entirely. Bobby didn't see her as the average female. He saw her as an equal and she meant to keep it that way.

In the meantime, she was game for any and everything that kept her busy and out of sight until tonight, regardless of whether it was waiting for a delivery at Honey's, or driving over to the next town to pick up something to wear tonight. And a red velvet cake. Just in case.

"I'm headed out to run a few errands that Matt left unfinished," she told Bobby a few minutes later. "I'll be on my radio if you need me."

To HELL WITH *slow and steady.*

The thought struck when Shelly opened the door later that night and Colton got a really good look at her—from her long, gleaming brown hair flowing sexy and loose past her shoulders, to her pink-tipped toes stuffed into high-heeled sandals.

And everything in between.

The dress she wore was short and tight, cut down to *there* and up to *here.* Hot pink spandex hugged her voluptuous curves and spelled a very detailed picture that left little to the imagination. Not that he needed one where she was concerned. He'd seen every inch of her incredible body, touched it, tasted it.

More.

Lust sizzled and popped inside of him and his gut twisted. His gaze shifted down, drinking in the picture she made, savoring it, before sweeping back up.

At least, he tried for a clean sweep, but his attention seemed hell-bent on pausing at several interesting spots along the way.

The long, bare legs that seemed to go on endlessly.
The flare of her hips. The press of her ripe nipples
beneath the thin material of her dress. The deep vee
between her luscious breasts. The bare curve of one
shoulder. The frantic beat of her pulse. The smooth
column of her throat. Her full, pink lips.

Need rolled over him and his hands trembled,
eager to pull her close and feel her ripe mouth so
soft and pliant beneath his own.

A kiss, of all things. He wanted another friggin'
kiss.

He stiffened and gave himself a fierce mental ass-
kicking. Ruthless vampires didn't crave kisses. Not
even desperate ones. They wanted sex. Energy. Satisfaction.

Get it together, Braddock. Fast.

He wasn't going to waste time kissing Shelly Lancaster because if he kissed her now, he'd sure as hell
want to do it again and again and again. Tonight
would be shot to hell and back before it had even
gotten started.

No, he wasn't getting that close. At least not yet.

"I've been waiting for you." Her soft voice slid
into his ears and swept along his nerve endings. She
drew a deep breath. Her full breasts heaved. The
dress tugged and pulled in all the right places and
his gut twisted.

He narrowed his gaze, determined to resist the
sudden urge to push her up against the nearest wall

and bury himself hilt deep inside of her, which was exactly what she wanted.

She wanted it now. Over.

One night.

He forced his attention away from her decadent body. His gaze lifted and collided with hers, and damned if the heat in her rich chocolate eyes didn't sucker punch him as much as the sight of her in that slinky, sexy number.

He frowned. "Why are you dressed like that?"

"This old thing?" She shrugged one bare shoulder. "I just grabbed the first thing when I heard the door. Do you like it?"

"It's a little skimpy." He meant the comment as a criticism, to stir her insecurity and put some much needed distance between them.

Instead, her cheeks rosied and a smile touched her lips. As if he'd said just the right thing.

"Really?" She glanced down. "I was worried that it might not be short enough."

"Short enough for what?"

"For the three B's." Before he could ask, she waved a hand. "Don't ask. Just come on in." She pulled open the door and motioned him inside. Hunger flashed in her gaze. "It's time."

He caught the door frame before his legs could waltz right on in. "It's a really nice night." He glanced behind him. "Let's go out."

Disappointment flashed in her gaze, followed by

the briefest rush of fear. Because Shelly Lancaster didn't do relationships anymore than he did.

But this wasn't even close. He wasn't the least bit anxious to get to know her. Not her past or her present or her hopes and dreams. The only thing Colton gave a flip about were the physical nuances that made the chemistry burn so hot between them. The way she trembled and sighed when he touched her just so. The way her cheeks went pink and glowing when she exploded against his mouth. The way her eyes turned a deep, dark, liquid chocolate when she wanted him inside of her.

At least that's what he told himself.

"Listen," she said when he reached for her hand. "I think it's really important that we keep things in perspective. I mean, it's not that I don't like you. I don't really know you, which is exactly the point. I don't need to know you. This isn't about me liking you or you liking me. We're not dating." She voiced the fear in her eyes.

He smiled. "Sugar, this isn't a date." He leaned in and let his lips brush the shell of her ear. Heat zipped up and down his spine and his groin tingled. "It's foreplay."

13

"THIS CAN'T BE THE right place," Shelly said fifteen minutes later when Colton pulled the pick-up truck into the parking lot of the local fairgrounds and killed the engine.

Welcome to the twenty-first annual Skull Creek chili cook-off and hot dog eating competition!

Shelly read the words that blazed up on the lit marquis in front of the ten acre dirt parking lot and a wave of apprehension went through her. While it was only Thursday and the real fun didn't start until tomorrow, when Mark Burris and Mitchell Sutherland went head-to-head to see who could stuff the most weenies into their mouth without puking first, the two dozen competition chili teams had already fired up their trucks for the preliminary round of cooking. Tonight would narrow things down to the top five who would go all out on Saturday for first place.

With a whopping five extra teams entered this year, the turn-out was even bigger than expected.

Guilt swamped her and she barely resisted the urge
to hop out and start doing a little crowd control. She
should be here, keeping an eye on things, doing her
job.

Cars and pick-ups overflowed the gravel parking lot, spilling into a nearby field where she caught
a glimpse of Bobby directing traffic with his light
wand. When he glanced in her direction, she pulled
the edges tighter on the duster she'd grabbed before
leaving the house. She sunk lower into her seat and
damned herself for falling for Colton's ploy.

She'd envisioned a dozen scenarios when she'd
climbed into the shiny black truck. Everything from
a dimly lit restaurant complete with oysters on the
half shell and an acoustic guitar player, to a bottle of
champagne and a box of chocolates down by the lake.

Something seductive. Sexy. The perfect aphro-
disiac.

But this?

This was a date, plain and simple, and Shelly Lancaster didn't do dates.

In the middle of the fairgrounds, a live band belted
out a tune from Blake Shelton while people two-
stepped across a make-shift sawdust floor. A ring
of cooking trailers surrounded the perimeter. The
smell of chili powder and cayenne pepper filled the
air and teased her nostrils.

Off to the left, a few carnival rides had been set
up for the kids, including a merry-go-round, a Ferris
wheel and a gigantic bouncy castle. To the right, a

concession stand offered up quart-size cups of beer from a local sponsor. A margarita machine *whirred,* churning out icy drinks.

"There is nothing sexy about chili. Except for Ben Avery." When he arched an eyebrow, she added, "He's the reigning champion. When he isn't winning local competitions with his infamous *Chili From Hell*, he works as a ranch hand."

"And you like ranch hands?"

"Not specifically, but I can appreciate an impressive backside and a pair of rocking abs as much as the next woman."

He stiffened and she had the insane feeling that he was actually jealous. But a man had to care to be jealous and Colton Braddock wasn't the caring type. He'd made that much perfectly clear.

Her mind traveled back to the previous night to the feel of his lips on her neck, her shoulders, her breasts—sex. This was all about sex and Colton Braddock was just what she needed.

But was she what *he* needed? She was starting to wonder. While he'd made the offer himself, it was obvious he was dragging his feet for some reason. Had he changed his mind?

She stiffened and turned accusing eyes on him. "I think we should go back to my place, unless there's some reason you don't want to." She held his stare. "If you've changed your mind, that's fine. Just spit it out."

"Come on." A wicked smile spread across his lips. "It'll be fun."

"I thought we were going for sexy, not fun."

"There's nothing wrong with both." The grin faded from his lips as he eyed her. "What is it you're so afraid of?"

"Nothing," she blurted, because Shelly didn't do fear any more than she did dates. "I just don't think this is the appropriate place to do this." Especially since she was wearing her Triple B dress. Great for private seductions. Not so great for prancing around in front of half the town. She had an image to maintain, after all. A professional, no-nonsense, let's kick butt image that served her well as the Deputy Sheriff of Skull Creek.

She certainly wasn't hesitating because the last time she'd worn a dress had been at her high school graduation when Marcus Sawyer had told her she looked weird.

"You look great." Colton's deep voice pushed into her thoughts and if she hadn't known better, she would have sworn he saw right through her.

Into her.

One callused finger touched a tendril of hair and pushed it back behind her ear. "You don't look weird at all," he murmured and then he climbed from behind the wheel before she could blurt out *What the hell?*

The hair on the back of her neck prickled as he rounded the front of the truck. The door creaked and suddenly he was standing there, his hand out-stretched, a challenging light in his eyes as he waited for her to make the next move.

Beautiful.

The word echoed through her head and where she would have refused any other man, there was something oddly compelling about his voice.

For a split second, she forgot everything except the way the deep timbre vibrated along her nerve endings. He really did have a great voice. And he definitely said all the right things. As if he saw deep down inside of her and knew just how to punch her buttons.

As if he cared.

The thought was like a reality check and she stiffened. "Where did the weird comment come from?" she asked, calling him out the way she should have a few moments ago.

He looked surprised, but then the expression dived straight into a blank look. He shrugged. "You seem dead set on covering up and I know how sensitive women can be."

Not because he knew her, but because he knew women. All women. She had no doubt he'd been with more than his share. His expertise last night had proved as much. He'd brought her to the brink with his practiced hands and purposeful movements, and so the explanation made sense.

At the same time, she couldn't shake the feeling that something didn't add up.

Something about him.

"It's a little warm out tonight." His deep voice killed any more internal speculation and she glanced down at the duster belted securely at her waist. "You sure you don't want to leave that in the truck?"

Um, no. "There's a cold front coming through and I want to be ready." She made a big show of shivering.

"It's the middle of July."

"Yeah, well, you know what they say about Texas. If you don't like the weather, wait five minutes."

He eyed her for a long moment. "You don't have to hide who you really are for people to respect you."

"It's called projecting an air of professionalism, and spandex isn't professional. Not that that's why I'm wearing the coat. The Sheriff's department gets a head up on all extreme weather changes." She tucked a strand of hair behind her ear and tried to ignore the sweat already trickling between her shoulder blades. "The temperature is supposed to drop just like that." A sliver of guilt worked its way through her, but she shrugged it off.

The temperature *was* going to drop.

Only eight degrees, but that was beside the point. Bottom line—it was going to be cooler than it was right now. "I hope you brought a jacket."

"The cold doesn't really bother me."

Again she felt a trickle of apprehension, as if they were talking about more than just the weather. "Suit yourself. But don't come crying to me when you're freezing your buns off."

"Sugar, there's enough heat between us to give hell a run for its money. Freezing buns aren't even a remote possibility."

His deep voice stirred and teased. Excitement zipped up her spine, swamping the apprehension until her nerves buzzed.

She drew a shaky breath, suddenly desperate for more air as he took her hand and guided her forward.

"So what's the plan," she asked as they reached the line to get in. "Making out in the bathroom? Groping each other on the Ferris wheel? Going to third base under the bleachers?" The smell of spicy, bubbling chili teased her nostrils and her stomach grumbled, reminding her she'd been so frantic to get an outfit together that she hadn't had time to eat dinner.

"Easy." He grinned. "Why don't we grab some chili and see which one is the best?"

"I thought this was about foreplay?"

"Eating chili *is* foreplay."

"Maybe to an evening spent in the bathroom. I'd rather do more damage in the bedroom."

He grinned. "Foreplay is all about stimulating the senses." He breathed in. His nostrils flared and his gaze sparked. "Just let the place work its magic."

She became acutely aware of the smells teasing her nostrils, the sounds playing at her ears, the bright lights widening her eyes. He was right and suddenly there seemed to be nothing wrong with a little eating and talking and getting to know each other.

In the name of foreplay, of course.

"I *am* a little hungry."

He winked. "Then let's start playing, sugar."

14

"WE'VE GOT YOUR turkey chili, venison chili, vegetarian chili, green chicken chili, white bean chili, chili con carne and chili from hell." Alice Winkle, owner of the local diner and chairman of this year's cook-off, motioned to the array of steaming bowls sitting on the counter in front of her. "Pick your poison," she told Colton.

"The green chicken chili sounds good." And smelled even better. While Colton couldn't grab a spoon and dig in, he could still enjoy the experience. A vampire's sense of smell was extremely heightened. One good whiff of the delicious chili as a vampire would be more satisfying than eating an entire bowl as a human. "What about you?" Colton turned to Shelly.

"Oh, she'll have her usual," Alice cut in, "ain't that right, Shelly?" The woman winked as she reached for a fiery looking bowl from the very end. "Shelly's the only one in town who can eat an entire bowl of *Chili from Hell* without taking a drink or going to the E.R."

When Colton arched an eyebrow, Shelly said, "I won the title last year in the chili-eating competition."

"That's right." Alice beamed. "She beat Harry Farnsworth and ended his ten year winning streak."

"Harry's the chief of the Cherrywood Police Department," Shelly added. "We sort of have this rivalry with them. Matt was supposed to do it last year, but he had a family function so I stepped in and took his place."

"And it's a good thing she did, otherwise we woulda lost like we did all those years before. But Shelly, here, ate the whole danged thing in two minutes and thirty-eight seconds, and now we've got the bragging rights." Alice beamed as she handed over the bowl. "Wait." She added an extra habanera on top. "There you go. Enjoy."

"You guys take your chili seriously," Colton said as they found a spot at a nearby picnic table.

"You should see us during the annual rib cook-off." She folded herself in across the table from him. She reached for the sleeve of crackers sitting at the center of the table next to a roll of paper towels. In a matter of seconds, she'd crumbled half the package into her bowl.

He arched an eyebrow. "Why do you do it?"

"Do what?" She took the first bite and grimaced.

"Fight so hard to keep up appearances."

"I already told you—I'm running for Sheriff when Matt retires. Reliability builds trust."

"It'll also drive you crazy if you do it for too long. You have to cut loose once in a while."

If only.

"That's what my Grandma Jean used to say." A light gleamed in her eyes and a small smile touched her lips. "Of course, she was talking about wearing a red scarf to church as opposed to a beige one, but still."

"A wise woman."

"She was. She knew everything from how to fix her own water heater to how to change the fuel pump on her truck. She said it was because of my Grandpa Ralph. I never knew him, but she said he was a good man. He was sick a long time and so he taught her how to do stuff so that she wouldn't have to depend on anyone. She tried to teach my mom the same, but she wasn't interested in learning how to do things for herself. Or anyone else for that matter. She liked going out a lot more than taking care of two little girls."

"That must have been tough."

"Not at first. We had my Grandma Jean, but then she passed away and my sister and I were left to fend for ourselves."

"How old were you?"

"I was six and my sister was three." Shelly hesitated, as if deciding just how much she wanted to tell him. "I didn't know what to do at first," she finally admitted. "But I learned how to set my own alarm clock and make a mean peanut butter and jelly sandwich." When he arched an eyebrow, she added, "I've never been much for cooking. Anyhow, I managed to take care of myself and my sister, and we made it. Meanwhile, my mom partied all night."

"How are things now?"

"She still lives in the same run-down trailer on the edge of town. Still going out all night and sleeping all day. I drop off groceries once a week and Darla stops by to check on her, but she's no more interested in us now than she was back then." Sadness gleamed in her gaze before she seemed to gather her composure and he had the crazy urge to reach out.

Because he knew how she felt. His own father hadn't given a rat's ass about him or his brothers.

But this wasn't about easing her conscience or soothing her worry. This was about sex. Which meant he wasn't going to touch her.

"That must be tough," he said instead.

"I can handle it." She stared pointedly at him. "What about you? Any dysfunctional parents lurking in your closet?"

He shrugged. "My parents died a long time ago. It's just me."

"And your brothers," she reminded him. "There are three, right?"

He nodded. "Cody's the youngest. Then Brent and Travis."

"Are you guys close?"

"We used to be." He meant to end the conversation there, but damned if the words didn't find a way out before he could stop them. "My dad left when I was really young and so I ended up riding shotgun over my brothers. They didn't like it most of the time, but they sure as hell needed it. They were into everything." He smiled. "And so was I. We did everything together."

"And now?"

His smile faded. "Times have changed." *He'd* changed. He'd failed them when they'd needed him most. He'd failed his own son. He shrugged. "We don't see each other much, what with me being in New Mexico and them being here."

"But you're here now, so you guys can get reacquainted."

If only. He stifled the sudden thought and shook his head. "It's not that simple."

"Sure it is. Just grab a pizza and catch up. That's what Darla and I do when we've both been busy to spend time together. We eat. We talk. She ends up painting my toenails and I end up lecturing her about her latest boyfriend. Just like that we're back to being besties."

She made it sound so simple, but then she didn't know the truth—that he was a vampire hell bent on revenge—and being *besties* didn't figure into the death and destruction that waited for him.

Getting close to his brothers would only make it hard on them when he finished with Rose and ended his own miserable existence. No, it was better to keep his distance.

That's what he told himself, but with Shelly sitting across from him, her eyes gleaming with encouragement, he wasn't so sure he believed it. She made it seem possible.

She made him actually want to try.

He killed the crazy notion and pushed to his feet. "Let's go."

She eyed his full bowl. "Don't you want to eat your chili?"

"Do you really want to eat yours?" he countered.

"I see your point." She followed his lead and snatched up the cracker-laden mess in front of her. "First one to the trash is a rotten egg."

FINALLY.

Shelly held tight to the realization as she wiped a drop of perspiration from her temple and followed Colton from the main tent. They were leaving.

No more curious glances. No more stifling heat. Soon she could shed the coat and breathe.

Even more, she could have sex. Hot, vibrant, toe-curling *sex.*

Her heart kicked up in anticipation and her steps quickened....

Until they bypassed the Exit leading to the parking lot and stopped in front of a monstrous wagon overflowing with hay bales.

"I thought we were going home." She watched in

disappointment as Colton pulled out a twenty and handed it over to the driver.

"I never said that." The troubled expression that had carved his features back at the table had faded and now he was back to being the wicked, irresistible bad boy. A grin tugged at his sensuous lips as he winked. "I was just saving you from a trip to hell."

"Says you." She eyeballed the two horses hooked up to the front of the wagon. "I grew up in a trailer park. I'm not much into horses."

"There's a first time for everything." He eyed her, challenge gleaming in his gaze. "Unless you're scared, that is."

Them's fightin' words.

At least to a girl who'd grown up trying to prove she was the exact opposite. To everyone around her, but most of all, to herself.

She squared her shoulders, gathered her courage and motioned him into the back of the wagon. "Lead the way."

15

SHELLY WATCHED AS Colton climbed into the back of the wagon. She did her best not to stare at his butt outlined by the skin-tight Wranglers, but it was right there. And she was so hot. And he was so perfect. And…*oh, my.*

He turned and caught her before she could look away. His mouth crooked into a grin as he held out his hand. "My turn to enjoy the view."

"There isn't much view from the front."

"Says you." He motioned to her coat which had slipped open just enough to give him a tantalizing view of her cleavage. He hoisted her up next to him. His hand lingered on hers. "Aren't you burning up yet?"

She swallowed. Hard. "No," she finally managed.

"Don't worry, sugar." He sat down on a nearby hay bale and pulled her next to him. "You will be."

With everyone gathered in the main arena for the upcoming chili tasting competition, the hay ride had been all but forgotten. They were the only two passengers as the driver yanked the reins and gave a quick "Giddyup."

The wagon jumped and the inch of space between them disappeared. Her thigh settled against his as they launched into a steady roll. The sound of music and laughter faded, giving way to the buzz of crickets and the creak of the wagon. Stars studded the velvety sky and the moon sat big and bold above them. Green pasture stretched in front of them and the mirrorlike surface of a nearby lake gleamed in the distance.

Seconds ticked by and she found herself leaning into Colton, lulled by the steady rocking and the peaceful tranquility of the warm Texas night. She felt so far away from everyone and everything.

Fat chance.

The wagon moved at the pace of a turtle and so they were still within earshot when a high-pitched giggle drew her attention. She glanced at two teenage girls who stood on the edge of the fairgrounds. One of them waved, a knowing gleam in her eyes as she shifted her attention to Colton for a brief second and then back to Shelly. She nudged her friend and pointed.

Reality rained down on Shelly and she gave herself a great big mental slap. What the hell was she doing?

She was glued to Colton's side. Practically cuddling, of all things. Before she knew it, they'd be gazing at the stars and sharing their hopes and dreams.

Like how much she wanted to run for Sheriff and how terrified she was of losing. And how she was even more terrified of giving in to the passion blazing inside of her and winding up a slave to it. Just like her mother.

She stiffened, the motion pulling her shoulder away from his and giving her a blessed inch of distance. "I'm still not getting the foreplay aspect of any of this," she said with tight lips.

This wasn't sexy.

No, this was downright romantic, and God help her, but she liked it. She *liked* it.

"You don't have to be so uptight."

She half turned to see him staring at her, into her, as if he could see all of her secrets. "Uptight?" Her gaze narrowed. "It's called being alert, and this is how I am all the time. But then you wouldn't know that because you don't know me very well."

"Ah, but I do." He rested a hand atop her knee and his fingers moved under the hem of her coat until he felt bare skin. "I know you're anxious to get off this wagon because it makes you uncomfortable."

"I don't like to waste time and I just don't see the point to this."

"That's because you're not using your imagination." His expression grew dark and serious and hungry. "If you want to have really great sex, you've got to have a great buildup." A tiny pinpoint of light gleamed in the center of his eyes. "You have to feed the fire until it burns up everything. Your common sense. Your inhibitions. Your fear." Before she could protest, he leaned in and touched his lips to hers in an urgent kiss that sparked the heat already zinging through her body.

Heat that had nothing to do with the warm night air and the coat she was wearing, and everything to do with the passion blazing inside her. Her heart skipped a few beats and anticipation sizzled along her nerve endings.

His hand slid up the inside of her thigh. Slow. Steady. Purposeful.

The air choked in her throat as his finger grazed the slit between her legs. She stiffened and her gaze swiveled from the steadily disappearing fairgrounds to the driver sitting up front.

No one can see. That's what she told herself, her need warring with a lifetime of fear and uncertainty. There wasn't a soul in sight except the driver and he was busy with the horses. No one was looking at them and even if they were, all they would see is Colton's arm partially concealed by her coat. They wouldn't know that she wasn't wearing panties or that he was stroking her or that she *wanted* him to stroke her.

"Don't think about them," Colton murmured in her ear a heartbeat before his fingertip found her slit. He traced the delicate line before dipping inside just a fraction. She gasped and her gaze locked with his.

"Think about what I'm doing to you. What you want me to do to you."

Desire gleamed hot and bright in his eyes, but there was something else, as well. Surprise. Admiration. Respect. As if he'd never seen a woman like her, or wanted one quite so much.

Just like that, her inhibitions seemed to slip away and suddenly the only thing that mattered was the desperation coiling inside of her.

She relaxed and her legs parted in silent invitation.

He dipped a finger into her steamy heat and slid inside slowly.

So tantalizingly *slow.*

Her eyes closed and she would have toppled backward if he hadn't caught her.

A split-second later, she found herself sitting on the hay bale in front of him, his thighs framing hers, her back flush against his chest.

The fairgrounds had all but faded from view, but she no longer cared. She was too aware of him—too desperate for him—to put up a fight when he unbelted the coat and parted the edges. The wool slid free and blessed air rushed over her bare arms and shoulders.

"This is much better." He slid an arm around her waist to hold her firmly in place while he swept a hand up the inside of her thigh. Higher. Higher. Until his thumb brushed the slick folds between her legs. "Don't you think?"

"I…"

He slid the tip of his finger into her and pleasure speared, hot and jagged, through her trembling body. She caught her bottom lip, biting down against the exquisite sensation.

"Yes," she finally managed, the word catching on another gasp as the wagon bounced and his finger slid a fraction deeper.

She tilted her head back and rested it in the curve of his shoulder as she surrendered to the ecstasy beating at her sanity.

He knew just how to touch her, how to push deep until the air lodged in her throat and her senses flooded with sensation. Meanwhile, the wagon rumbled along. The rocking motion fed the intensity of what was happening and increased the pressure.

Winding her tighter.

Pushing her closer.

There.

She braced her hands on his thighs, her fingers digging into the hard muscle as the first vibration hit her.

When he slid a second finger inside of her, she came apart. Shudders vibrated through her body, skimming along her ragged senses in wave after wave of sweet, decadent sensation.

She slumped back against him, weak and damp, her breath raspy, her heartbeat a frenzied rhythm in her chest. His strong arms closed around her, holding her close as if he never meant to let her go.

She knew better.

This was sex and there would be an end to it even though they still hadn't made it to the main event. That was next judging by the rock-hard erection pressing against her.

It would end, all right. He would walk away and she would be glad, and it would be business as usual.

But in the meantime...

She closed her eyes and settled against him.

This was nice.

At least until the ride ended and Bobby found her, frantic with the news that she'd better come quick because all hell was breaking loose back at the jail.

16

"THIS IS BAD," Shelly said as she stood in the outer office near the dispatch counter and stared at the woman on the security monitor.

Honey Gentry sat on her bunk, her hair wild, her eyes puffy and red. Her nose was swollen and running. Tears streamed down her face and mascara streaked her cheeks. It looked as if a tornado had whipped through the room. Feathers littered the floor courtesy of the busted pillow in the far corner. The blanket that had covered the bunk was now in shreds. Honey sat in the middle of it all, frantically tying the ends of the blanket shreds into one long rope.

Uh-oh.

The only upside was that she barely had twelve inches. It wasn't nearly enough to loop over the bars and do anything stupid.

Not yet anyway.

"Woman scared the bejesus out of me," Truitt

said, drawing Shelly's attention to the Ranger standing near the coffeemaker.

As if he'd be any place else.

"One minute I was sitting there doing my crossword," he continued, "and the next, I'm running for my life."

"Did she threaten you?"

"Hell, no. Ain't no little gal gonna threaten me. The dadburned female busted out crying." He gave a visible shudder. "I only put up with one crying woman and only 'cause she lets me have the remote the other three weeks of the month."

Shelly shook her head and turned to John. "How long has she been like this?"

"Since about three. Ever since Millie over in Judge Meyers's office called and said he wasn't going to make it back at all today."

"Another flat?"

"He ran out of gas."

"I swear that man needs a Triple A membership." Shelly punched a button and the camera panned in, giving them an up-close look at Honey and her bloodshot eyes.

Bobby and John gasped. *Men.*

She scanned the camera down, searching for any sort of weapon. While Honey had shred the blanket, she seemed to have done it with her bare hands. After a few seconds scanning the cell's interior, Shelly straightened and caught John giving her an odd look.

She became keenly aware of Colton who stood

nearby, one hip planted on her desk. His muscular arms were folded, his pale eyes hooked on her. Awareness rippled through her and she fought against the sensation.

"What?" she snapped at John, determined to keep her mind focused. This was work and she wasn't going to think about what she was going to do with Colton after work. *Focus.* "You've never seen a woman wearing a trench coat before?"

"Actually, I've never seen *you* wearing a trench coat before." His gaze dropped. "Or a dress. Or high heels for that matter." He swallowed. "I didn't even know you had high heels."

"You'd never catch a Texas Ranger wearing high heels, lemme tell ya," Truitt chimed in, reaching for another foam cup.

Shelly tamped down on a sudden rush of insecurity and glared. "That stuff doesn't come cheap, you know." She motioned to the jar sitting next to the machine. "If you're going to guzzle coffee like that, you need to start chipping in with everyone else." She squared her shoulders, pulled the belt tighter and turned toward the containment area. "I'm going in."

"Not alone, you aren't." Colton was right behind her.

His muscular chest kissed her shoulder blades before she could make it two steps and heat zig-zagged through her. She stiffened and kept walking. "I'm more than capable of handling this."

"I have no doubt. But the department didn't institute a buddy rule regarding dangerous situations for the fun of it." He motioned to one of the numerous posters lining the wall behind Bobby's desk, detailing specifics of dealing with various situations. From first response to containment.

The first rule of any situation? *Always call for backup.* "That's *backup*, meaning another officer." Shelly paused at the security door and eyeballed Bobby. "How about it?"

Bobby took one look at the monitor and shook his head. "If it's a fire fight, I'm right behind you. But my Xbox doesn't simulate hormonal women."

"Coward." Her gaze shifted to John.

He shrugged. "I got two kids to think of."

She turned to Truitt.

"Forget it. It ain't my problem." He glared and dropped a quarter into the jar before taking a sip of his coffee. "I'm on special assignment with Holbrook."

Colton shrugged. "Looks like you're stuck with me."

"Fine then." She blew out an exasperated breath. "But just stay back and let me handle things." She powered open the door.

A moment later, they were inside. Following protocol, she locked the outer door before punching in the code to unlock Honey's cell. The metal groaned and clicked.

"Honey?" She slid open the cell door and took a tentative step inside.

The woman's head snapped up and her eyes lit with a crazed light. "Sssssshhhhhhhh." She motioned to Holbrook's cell. He lay on his side, eyes closed, facing them. "Don't you dare wake him." She shook her head frantically. "I won't be able to take it if you wake him up. He'll start exercising again and I'll go crazy." She shook her head frantically. "I tried, Shelly. I tried not to look, but I can't help myself. He's got so many muscles and this cell is so small and it's been so long since I—" The words cut off as he stirred, rolling over onto his back.

Honey held a finger to her lips, her eyes pleading.

Seconds ticked by and then the soft, steady sound of his snores filled the silence.

"He's still asleep," Shelly mouthed. "I'm coming in." She moved toward Honey, eyeballing every corner of the cell, drinking in her surroundings before her gaze shifted back to the woman. "What are you making?"

"It's a rope."

"Listen…" Shelly sat down on the edge of the bunk. "I know you're upset, but nothing is worth doing something like this."

"You haven't been stuck in this cell for two days."

"No, but I've been in stressful situations before. I know what it's like to feel hopeless. Like you have nowhere to turn. But you do have somewhere to turn. You turn to yourself. You draw on your own strength. And you get through it. You don't give up and hang yourself."

Honey's head snapped up and her gaze locked with Shelly's. "Is that what you think I'm trying to do?"

"Isn't it?"

"Hardly." The woman gave a hysterical giggle before the sound faded and sheer desperation filled her expression. "My lipstick rolled under Ranger Truitt's chair," she said as if she'd just declared the end of the world was coming.

"What?"

"The lipstick you let me borrow." She motioned frantically and Shelly turned to catch a glimpse of gold amid the litter of foam cups. "I accidentally dropped it and it rolled and that can't happen because I need it before he wakes up." She touched her face. "I look a mess. It's no wonder he isn't paying me any attention. But if I get that lipstick, it'll be different." She held up the pitiful excuse for a rope, "See, I figured I'd loop this over the chair and drag it over…" Her words faded as she seemed to think. "You could get it for me," she blurted, grabbing the lapels of Shelly's coat. "Would you do that?"

Shelly realized then that Honey wasn't a woman on the verge of suicide. She was a woman about to spontaneously combust of sexual frustration.

She knew the feeling.

Despite the orgasm during the hay ride, she still felt anxious. Needy. Desperate. She wanted more.

Boy, did she ever.

"Would you get the tube for me?" Honey's desperate voice drew her back to the moment. "I need it now. I really do. *Please*."

"Forget the lipstick." She took the woman by the hand. "We're getting out of here." While she couldn't solve her own problem and force Colton into bed with her, she could help Honey out with hers.

"Really?" Honey turned hopeful eyes on Shelly.

"Really."

"But what about Judge Meyers? Isn't he the only one who can release me?"

"He's not here and I am. So let's go."

COLTON WATCHED Shelly slide an arm around the frantic woman's shoulders and steer her out of the cell. They'd made it two steps down the hallway before bedsprings creaked and a deep, male voice echoed off the walls.

"Don't tell me you're leaving without saying goodbye first."

Honey stalled and her head whipped back around, her gaze going straight to the man who'd stepped up to the cell door.

"I thought we were friends."

"I—" she protested, but Colton was already in front of her, his back to Holbrook, effectively blocking her view.

His gaze met hers and he sent the silent command. *Just keep walking*.

But it wasn't that easy. Honey was too far gone. She needed another look. She wanted one.

"We are friends. I just—"

"Move," Shelly added, determined to save the woman from herself. She started pushing and pretty soon, Honey was back in motion, headed for the security door.

"Don't I get a free pass, too?" Holbrook's voice drew Colton around just as Shelly powered open the door and pushed Honey through.

"Not this time," Colton said. "Not ever again—" The last word choked in his throat as he got his first good look at Jimmy Holbrook.

But it wasn't the man's resemblance to Rose that tied his gut into knots. No, it was the eyes staring back at him.

Eyes so familiar they could have been his own.

They *were* his own.

Colton's mind rushed back to that night, to the frantic search for CJ. He'd looked everywhere for the body, and he'd found it. A small boy. Burned beyond recognition, but still, he'd known. There had been no other children at the Circle B.

It had to have been CJ.

It *was*.

"Hey, man." Jimmy gave him a disarming smile. "Are you okay?"

He wasn't. He was crazy. Delusional. CJ had died that night. Colton had seen for himself.

He'd smelled the death.

He'd felt the pain.

No!

He moved so fast that he knew he was little more than a blur to Shelly and the other Deputies as he rushed from the containment area and left the Sheriff's office. He needed to get away. To get out there.

To get away from the unimaginable.

Before he actually started to believe that maybe, just maybe, he hadn't lost everything that night. That somehow, someway, his son had survived Rose's treachery, and Jimmy Holbrook was the living proof.

Like hell.

He fought the past as he climbed into his truck and hauled ass out of town. The engine roared and the metal shook as his tires ate up pavement. He needed to move faster, to outrun the vision that dogged him.

Holbrook's eyes.

His eyes.

It couldn't be true. He didn't want it to be true.

That would mean that he'd not only lost his son that night, but that his son had lost his father, as well. CJ would have grown up without *him*. *Without* the one man in his life he needed the most. Even more, he would have thought the worst—that Colton had abandoned him. His son would have learned to hate him the way he'd hated his own father. And he would have had every right.

Colton had been convinced his son was dead. He hadn't looked for him. He hadn't torn up every inch of countryside searching for the boy the way he should have.

No!

Colton had been able to live with his fatal mistake that night—showing up late when he should have been there early—but only because he'd known that someday he would find the killer and make things right. But abandoning his son? He could never make that right.

Ever.

Anguish welled up inside him, along with a rush of rage that gripped him so tightly, he shook with the force of it.

Rose didn't just owe *him* for that night.

She owed their son for all the years she'd robbed him of his father. That explained why she'd been busting Holbrook out of jail every time he wound up behind bars.

But it wasn't enough. It was too small a price to pay for what she'd done.

Anger churned his gut and his fingers tightened on the steering wheel.

She owed much, *much* more and he would make her pay. But there would be no waiting, biding his time. *Hell,* no. He wanted blood and he wanted it now.

Forget Skull Creek. He knew Rose would be coming from El Paso once she discovered Holbrook missing, and so Colton would pick up his stuff back at the barn and get the hell out of town. He would head for El Paso and get to Rose that much sooner.

And then he'd kill her.

He'd extract a pound of flesh for all the pain

she'd caused the people he'd loved. His friends. His mother. His son.

And what if she senses you first and sees you coming?

But Colton was through listening. There were a dozen things that could go wrong. He didn't care. He just needed to get his hands on her, to take out his anger once and for all, to rid himself of the pain and suffering that pushed and pulled inside of him.

A haze of red clouded his vision as he drove toward the barn. Urgency pounded through him, so fierce and consuming that he almost missed the swirl of lights in his rearview mirror.

Almost.

But the blue cut through the haze and reality zapped him. And just like that, he felt the hitch in his chest. The frantic pounding of her heart. The ragged breaths rushing past her lips. The uneasiness urging her faster.

Shelly.

He knew it was her, even though the police car was too far away for him to see who was behind the wheel. He'd drank from her twice now and so the connection was stronger than before. He felt her. Her frustration and anxiety and fear, for him rather than herself.

Because she was falling for him the way he'd fallen for her.

Crazy.

She was friggin' crazy for feeling anything for him. And he was even crazier for wanting her to.

The minute the notion struck, he drop-kicked it right back out the door. No, he sure as hell was not falling for her, and she wasn't falling for him. And he had every intention of keeping it that way.

The only thing he wanted from her was sex. Blood.

Sustenance.

That's all she was to him. All she could ever be because Colton Braddock wasn't some cowboy she could take home to her family or show off at the weekly church picnic.

He was a vampire. A *vampire*.

He clenched his teeth, feeling the sharpness of his fangs cut into his tongue. The salty sweet taste of blood slid down his throat and firebombed in his empty stomach. He damned himself a thousand times for not bending her over that hay bale and working her out of his system when he'd had the chance.

He didn't need Shelly. He needed to drink her blood. To nurture his strength. To *do* something now when he'd done nothing back then.

He slammed on the brakes, swerved the truck onto the shoulder and killed the engine.

It was time to remember who and what he really was, to feed the beast that lived and breathed inside of him.

Starting right now.

17

SHE WAS WRITING him one hell of a ticket.

Speeding.

Public endangerment.

Failure to stop at a designated cattle crossing.

The charges ticked off in Shelly's head as she eased up behind his truck and shoved her cruiser into Park.

Violating curfew.

Reckless operation of a moving vehicle.

Walking out on her without so much as a goodbye.

Okay, so that last one wasn't against the law, but it pissed her off nonetheless. She'd barely even caught a glimpse as he'd hightailed it out of the office. No *goodbye.* Or *thanks for a lovely evening.* Not even a *see ya.* She'd barely had time to ask John to take Honey home before she jumped in her car to follow him.

Just who the hell did he think he was?

She held tight to the anger and climbed out, desperate to ignore the worry that roiled inside of her. The niggling sensation that told her something was wrong.

Deep down, she knew there was a problem, she just didn't know what it was. But then he stepped out of his truck and caught the glare of her headlights and she stopped dead in her tracks.

Disbelief pumped through her body at an alarming rate as she drank in the sight of him, her gaze riveted on his face, on his eyes that glowed a vivid, mesmerizing *purple*.

She blinked once, twice, but the color didn't fade into the pale, translucent blue that reminded her of a rain-washed sky on a hot summer's day.

Denial beat through her as the color seemed to shimmer and change. Right before her eyes, they fired a brilliant neon blue, so bright that it actually hurt to look at them.

Not that she could look away. Not with his lips drawn back and his fangs glittering and—

Wait a second.

Wait just a friggin' *second*.

Her heart pounded, echoing in her head, drowning out the steady *beep, beep, beep* of the car door she'd left wide open.

"Mama bear, you copy?" Bobby's voice carried over the radio, slicing through the noise, begging her to turn and climb back in. Respond. *Run.* "You took off outa here like a bat out of hell. What's wrong?"

Fangs. That's what was wrong. He had *fangs*.

Shock hit her like a thunder bolt and she clamped her eyes shut. The air rushed from her lungs and every muscle in her body froze.

No way.

No how.

It had to be lack of sex. That was it. The frustration had finally driven her completely off the deep end. Because there was no way she'd just seen...

That he actually had...

No.

Denial rushed through her, followed by a wave of panic when she opened her eyes again to see him still standing there, looking as ferocious as ever, his gaze still a blinding neon blue, his fangs still glittering in the headlights.

Still a *vampire*.

No. No. No.

There was no such thing. Vampires didn't exist. Only in books and movies and the minds of about a billion *Twilight* fanatics. But they were wrong.

Or were they?

The question beat at her as Bobby's voice blared in the background. "I've got you on GPS. I'm sending a squad car after you. Mama bear, you copy? Shelly?"

"Now you know what I am," Colton murmured, his deep voice slicing through the sound of her frantic heartbeat, drawing her full attention.

"No. You're a security specialist," she insisted. He shook his head and she pressed on. "A rancher."

"Actually, I am a rancher. But I'm also more." His

gaze fired brighter, changing colors again. "Much more."

"This isn't happening. There's no way you're a…" The word stalled on the tip of her tongue and she shook her head. "You're not. This is all some hoax."

"I am," he told her, his gaze pushing into hers. *I'm a vampire.* The deep timbre of his voice whispered through her mind, but his lips didn't move.

"Bullshit," she said, shaking her head frantically.

"You can't deny what you see. What you hear. What you *feel*." Just like that the belt of her robe tugged loose and she glanced up to see him staring at the material, moving it with nothing more than the sheer power of his gaze.

"It's part of who I am. I can control things with my mind. Move objects. Mesmerize people."

She grabbed at the ends, but they slipped from her grasp as if there were hands pushing at hers.

The truth crystallized as she felt the strong, purposeful touches and the brush of his rough skin against her own. And all while he stood several feet away, his muscles tight, his body immobile, his attention fixated on her.

He was a vampire.

A real, honest-to-goodness *vampire*.

A burst of excitement went through her, followed by a ripple of fear that made her hands tremble. Not because she was afraid of him. If he was really a vampire and that was a big *if,* he could have hurt her many times before now. He hadn't.

No, it wasn't Colton who stirred the fear.

It was her reaction to him. The excitement. The urge to rip off the coat and throw herself into his arms, despite the truth staring back at her.

Because of it.

Because she was weak and she didn't care about the consequences. She was lost in the moment, a slave to her own needs.

Just like her mother.

Suddenly she grabbed at the material harder, forcing the edges together, fighting that much harder. No way had Shelly spent a lifetime trying to distance herself from her past only to wind up right back where she'd started. Back under the bed, powerless to stop what was happening around her. Right in front of her.

"You believe me," he murmured.

"I most certainly do not."

"Yes, you do. It's true and you know it. You just don't want to admit it."

"The only thing I know is that you're in a shitload of trouble." She managed to tie the belt back into a knot only to have it slip through her fingers again and come undone.

He lifted his hand and the material rushed from her shoulders. And just like that, she stood before him wearing nothing but her Three B's dress and a tight frown.

"Forget all of the old myths. I don't have any sort of an aversion to garlic or crosses or holy water.

Silver can be painful, but not deadly. I'm pretty much immune to everything except for sunlight and stakes."

"And I can fly like Tinkerbell."

"I feed off both blood and sex," he continued, ignoring her skepticism. "They're both forms of energy that I use to survive, though if I'm having a lot of sex, I can take it easy on the blood and vice versa. And when I drink from someone, it forges a connection." *That's why you can hear me. And I can hear you.*

He couldn't.

That's what she told herself, despite the pieces which had already started to fall into place. The way his eyes changed color. The way he seemed to disappear in the blink of an eye. His overwhelming sex appeal.

She fought against the sudden sizzle of excitement that rushed through her and held tight to the denial.

"I came here because a woman—my ex-wife— set fire to my ranch one hundred and fifty years ago. She killed my family," he stated. "Right now, she's headed for Skull Creek and I intend to kill her when she arrives. That's why I'm here. She took everything from me. Everyone."

"But your brothers aren't dead," Shelly heard herself say as if she were buying this.

She wasn't. He was delusional and the whole coat thing was some kind of magic trick and—

"They were the only survivors," he added, ending her tirade as he went on one of his own, answering the multitude of questions that swam in her brain. "They were turned—I was turned—by a vampire who happened along that night. But Sawyer made a mistake. He turned the murderer, as well. That's why she's still out there—"

"Sawyer," she asked. "As in *Garrett Sawyer?*"

He nodded and the tidbits of information she knew about the man behind one of the South's largest custom motorcycle shops flashed in her brain. Garrett, who worked only at night. Garrett, who had a ranch that could double as a fortress. Garrett, who donated to every charity in town, but kept to himself despite numerous invites to attend this or that event. Garrett, who'd bitten and turned the woman who'd murdered Colton's family. Garrett the friggin' *vampire*.

"He didn't mean to turn her, but I'm glad he did. Otherwise I wouldn't have this chance." His gaze locked with hers and his eyes fired a furious red. "I'm going to make her pay for what she did. I *have* to make her pay." In a heartbeat, he was on her, his muscular body pinning her against the pick-up truck. Regret flashed in his gaze, taking a nose-dive into determination as he stared down at her. "I should have done this a long time ago."

"What are you doing?" she blurted, but she knew.

She saw the hunger in his gaze, felt it in his body, and a wave of apprehension washed through her.

"Feeding," he growled, confirming her worst fear. And then he kissed her.

18

THIS WAS WHAT she'd been waiting for.

He kissed her, plunging his tongue inside her mouth to explore and savor until she gasped for breath. He tasted so dark and dangerous and forbidden, and she soon found herself caught up in it. Eve in the Garden of Eden.

Her fear melted away and she forgot that she was standing on the side of the road in full view of anyone who happened by, totally mindless of Bobby's frantic voice telling her that John was on his way.

She didn't care about anything as she gave in to temptation. Her own longing boiled over and she kissed him back.

Even knowing that he was a vampire.

Because of it.

Forget good, old-fashioned chemistry. What flowed between them went beyond the ordinary, into the *extra*ordinary.

Lust rolled off of him in huge waves, courtesy of

his vampness, and she couldn't help but succumb to it. Any woman would have. He'd told her so himself. He could seduce with little more than a glance, brainwash with a sexy, seductive smile and hypnotize with a simple thought.

"Not you," he murmured against her lips before pulling away and staring down at her. "I can mesmerize any woman out there." He shook his head as if he still couldn't believe it. "But not you." His words sent a rush of warmth through her. "You're different."

Right. He was a vampire who craved both blood and sex. She could have been any woman.

But at that moment, she felt like *the* woman.

His, and his alone.

The lust that burned inside of her boiled over. She was powerless to resist him and oddly enough, that realization didn't freak her out nearly as much as it should have.

She wanted to feel him, to please him, to make him burn for her the way she burned for him. He made her feel hot and bothered and beautiful.

Her skin still tingled from the reverent way he'd stroked her on the hay ride. No man had ever looked at her like that.

It was her turn.

She reached for the waistband of his jeans.

A groan rumbled from his throat as her fingertips trailed over the denim-covered bulge. She worked the zipper down, tugging and pulling until the teeth finally parted. The jeans sagged on his hips, and his erection sprang hot and greedy into her hands.

She traced the ripe purple head before sliding her hand down his length, stroking, exploring. His dark flesh throbbed against her palm and a wave of electricity sizzled through her. She licked her lips, suddenly eager to taste him.

Insane.

She knew it was, but she couldn't help herself. She didn't want to help herself.

Dropping to her knees, she smoothed her fingers down the dark perfection of his shaft and took him into her mouth. And then she proceeded to show him just how much she wanted this.

How much she wanted him.

HE SENSED THE sudden change in her, the surrender, even before he felt her tongue trace the ripe head of his erection.

He closed his eyes for a long moment and indulged himself. She felt so damned warm. So damned wet. So damned *right*.

Before he could dwell on the last thought, his ears perked. The distant groan of a motor sizzled in the air. His eyes snapped open and his head jerked around. There wasn't a light on the horizon, but he knew someone was coming.

So?

What do you care? You want this. You need this.

He'd waited for this moment, this pleasure, for far

too long. He couldn't stop just because someone was coming or because he knew she would never recover from the embarrassment of having her reputation shot to hell and back. What did he care?

He didn't.

That's what he told himself, but he reached for her shoulders anyway. "We can't do this here."

"We can."

"No." His hand cupped her chin and forced her gaze up to meet his. "We can't." He pulled her to her feet. In a flash, he fastened his jeans, killed the lights and slammed both car doors. Scooping her off her feet, he started to move, racing across the pastureland as fast as his vampire feet could carry him.

In less than a minute, they were over two miles away, inside the old dilapidated barn, the door closed behind them. In a flash, he backed her up against the nearest wall, determined not to take a moment to reflect on what had just happened.

He'd already wasted too much precious time.

He caught the neckline of her skimpy dress and pulled it down to her waist. Her luscious breasts spilled free. Dipping his head, he caught one rosy nipple between his teeth. He flicked the tip with his tongue before opening his mouth wider, drawing her in. He sucked hard until a moan vibrated up her throat. The sound fed the lust roaring in his veins.

Pressing one hard thigh between her legs, he forced her wider until she rode him. Her sweet heat rasped against the denim of his jeans, melting through the fabric, scorching him.

She gasped and a shudder ripped through her. He leaned back to see her trembling lips and her quivering breasts. Her pulse beat frantically at the base of her throat, teasing and taunting, begging for his attention.

His lips parted with a slow hiss and his cock throbbed.

But it wasn't about plunging deep and spilling himself inside of her. It was all about her pleasure, about soaking up the sweet heat of her orgasm.

He shifted, moving and rubbing, working her until she drenched the material between them. The scent of her arousal teased his nostrils and stirred his senses, making him want to be inside of her so bad that it hurt.

Crazy.

He caught her lips in a fierce kiss and plunged his hand between her legs. She was warm and wet and swollen. At the first touch of his fingers, she stiffened. A cry ripped past her luscious lips and just like that, she came apart at his fingertips.

A sizzling heat pulsed through her body and entered him at every point of contact—his hand between her legs, his mouth on hers, his thigh pressed intimately between hers. He drank in the replenishing energy, soaking it up, relishing the dizzying rush of life through his undead body.

But it wasn't enough.

Like hell.

It was all about the orgasm, he reminded himself. The woman's orgasm. That's all he needed to feel totally and completely satisfied. All he'd ever needed.

He sure as shootin' didn't need one of his own.

But he wanted one.

The truth beat at his brain and this time he didn't push it away. He couldn't. Not with her so soft and pliant against him and his own hunger waging a war with his control.

He wanted to plunge deep inside of her over and over until he came so much that his teeth ached. And then he wanted to pull her into his arms and never let her go.

The realization sent a burst of panic through him and he turned, lifting her onto the nearest hay bale. The position put her breasts just inches from his face and he didn't waste any time. He had to sate the beast and kill the crazy urges roiling inside of him.

He stepped between her parted legs, wedging her knees further apart, and caught one ripe nipple in his mouth. His fangs grazed the tender flesh around her areola and his groin tightened. Her nipple throbbed against his tongue as he sank into her just a hair and drew a few precious drops of blood. The salty sweetness sent a dizzying rush to his head. His insides clenched.

He slid his palms around to cup her ass as he tilted her forward, bringing her flush against him. He stroked his head along the length of her slit once, twice, and then he sank his fangs deep, drawing on her, praying that the blood would be enough to kill the need for her.

It wasn't.

The more he took, the more he wanted. He couldn't help himself. He plunged deep inside her delicious heat and just like that, he was home.

His heart beat a thunderous rhythm in his ears for those next few moments as pleasure swamped him. Intense. Consuming. All he could do was stand there and soak it up for a long moment. But then it subsided and need took its place.

The need to get closer. Deeper. *Now.*

He thrust into her, over and over as he drew on her nipple. Her delicious essence filled his mouth and the energy from her sudden climax surrounded his cock, seeping into him at every point where flesh met flesh as he spilled himself deep inside her.

It was the ultimate in fulfillment for a vampire, and it still wasn't enough.

Not the warm, succulent body grasping at him or the sweet essence pulsing in his mouth or the satisfaction that he'd spent himself.

The realization sent him scrambling backward. He snatched up his discarded jeans and yanked them on before walking to the far side of the barn. He needed some distance from her.

From the feelings pushing and pulling at him and the crazy thought that she was the one woman he wanted enough to spend the rest of his life with.

Life?

He didn't have a life to spend. He was a vampire, for Chrissake. No such luxury existed for him. He'd already lived one hundred and fifty years too many.

He'd survived for one reason alone—revenge.

And once he had it, his sole purpose for surviving would end,

He would end it.

He *would*. Even if the notion weren't half as appealing as it used to be.

He forced aside the thought and hit the light hanging above the small work bench he'd set up near his sleeping bag. The smell of sawdust filled his nostrils and chased away the sweet scent of the woman sitting several yards away, watching him.

He needed distance. A distraction.

He picked up the sander and slid it across the block of wood he'd started working on last night. Shavings fell at his feet and the motion eased his tight muscles just a hair.

He heard the rustle of hay as she climbed off the bale, the soft pad of footsteps as she retrieved his discarded shirt. In his peripheral vision, he saw her pull on the soft cotton and walk toward him, her legs sexy and bare, her hair long and flowing and wild.

His gut hollowed out and he worked that much harder, determined to concentrate on the task at hand.

It should have been easy now that he'd replenished his strength. He could feel the buzz through his veins, the rush of adrenalin. *Focus.*

"What are you doing?" Her voice sounded a heartbeat before she stepped up next to him.

"Nothing."

"It doesn't look like nothing," she said, her gaze on the block of wood, as if she were genuinely interested. "What is it?"

"I don't know yet." He shrugged. "I was thinking I might make a bookshelf. Or maybe a table." *Or maybe even a bench.* He killed the notion and focused on the steady movements up and down. "I used to do woodworking a long, long time ago." He wasn't sure why he told her. He didn't like to think about that part of his life—the time before that one terrible night—much less talk about it. But he needed something to drown out the pounding of his own heart. "I made the stock for Cody's first gun. And one for Brent. And Travis."

"How old were you when your dad left?"

"I was twelve."

"That's young."

"Six is young," he said, reminding her of her own childhood. "At twelve I was practically a man. Old enough to look after my brothers, that's for sure."

"They were lucky to have you. You've definitely got skill." Silence settled as she watched him work for the next few minutes. "I'll never forget this one time when I tried making a costume for Darla. She was going to be in the kindergarten Christmas pageant and she needed a white dress so that she could be an angel. It ended up being a disaster, but she didn't care. She loved it anyway. That made me even more determined to do what I needed to do. What my Grandma Jean would have wanted. She was a strong woman."

"You're a strong woman." The words were out before he could stop them, but suddenly he didn't care. While sex with her had been fantastic, this ran a close second. And damned if he could resist her any more now than he had a few moments ago. "The first table I ever made fell over on its side when my momma sat a platter of chicken on it."

A grin tugged at her mouth. "Sounds like some table."

"I gave it to her for her birthday. It had crooked corners and jagged edges. And one leg was shorter than the other."

"I bet she loved it anyway."

"She did." For the first time in a long time, he let the memory come. He saw his mother standing there, a smile on her face as she'd scooped up the chicken. As if it was no big deal that he'd ruined her special dinner. His chest hitched. "I miss her." He'd never said that aloud before and the realization stirred a rush of panic.

Because he shouldn't be saying it now.

He should be focused on that one night. On the pain and death he'd witnessed. And the revenge he would soon taste.

"I'm really sorry for your loss."

"Don't be. It was my own fault."

"I'm sure—"

"Of what?" he said. "You weren't there. You don't know what really happened. You don't know shit."

"I know you were a good son and a good brother."

"Once upon a time maybe." He shrugged. "But I was always so damned set on doing the right thing that I let it get in the way." The memories stirred, welling up inside him. Just like that, the floodgates opened and the words poured out. "We were on our way home from the war for the first time in four years. The first time. And what did I do? I insisted on detouring to Austin to report to General Briggs. He expected a report on our last raid and I was determined to give it to him. That took four and a half hours, plenty of time for my wife and her bastard lover to put a bullet in everyone at the ranch. Time for them to herd all the livestock into the barn and set it on fire." The flames blinded him and the smoke burned his nostrils. "Time for them to kill every living thing that I ever loved and ride away without looking back." Anger and hurt whirled inside of him. "I shouldn't have gone to Austin. If I had been there, it never would have happened. If I had just *been there*..."

The truth hung in the air for a long moment, staring back at him, taunting him. His gut clenched and his chest tightened. And then he felt her arms slide around his waist.

She didn't tell him it wasn't his fault or that he couldn't have known what would happen or that he had to stop blaming himself. She didn't say any of the things he'd heard time and time again from his brothers.

She didn't say anything.

And that said everything.

She understood there were some mistakes that a man just couldn't put behind him and so she simply held him. And surprisingly enough, the knot in his chest eased.

"Did I ever tell you why I went into law enforcement?" her voice was soft, soothing.

"We haven't exactly spent a lot of time talking." He felt her smile against his shoulder blade before the expression faded. He touched the wood again, smoothing the sander over it in a lulling motion that was almost as soothing as her voice.

"I tried to make dinner for the first time and I accidentally set fire to the curtains." Her soft hands settled over his, her warmth seeping into him as she followed his movements with the sander. "The fire department came, along with children's protective services. They wanted to know where my mom was and why I was home alone cooking."

"Why were you?"

"Because my mom hadn't come home for four days." Her hands trembled atop his. "She was passed out in her truck in the parking lot of a local bar, thanks to too much Jack Daniels."

"Did you tell them that?"

"I should have, but I didn't. I lied because the thought of being completely alone was even worse than being stuck with a sorry excuse for a mother. I told them she was helping with the bake sale down at the church. They didn't believe me but Jack Mercer—he was the Sheriff at the time—told them to leave me be. And they listened. Everybody listened when Sheriff Jack said something. They paid attention and that's what I wanted. I wanted people to pay attention to me. To actually *see* me."

The way my mother never did.

The silent thought rolled through his head, even though she didn't say the words. Awareness rippled up his spine and he felt the rush of insecurity that went through her. The pain. Because she knew what loss felt like. She'd experienced it every day of her life that she'd watched her mother walk away from her.

She knew what he felt. The fear. The self-doubt. The isolation.

He turned and stared into her eyes and at that moment, he knew the reason for the damnable hunger that still ate away inside of him. He wanted more than just Shelly's body and her blood.

He wanted her heart.

And she wanted his.

He knew it the moment he saw her gaze, so full of an emotion that she wouldn't admit any more than he would.

Because it wouldn't change anything.

They both knew it. She would go back to her life and run for Sheriff of Skull Creek and he would face off with Rose and do what he had to do to avenge his family and silence his demons once and for all.

No, love didn't mean shit in the end.

But right now… Suddenly it meant everything. And he intended to show her just how much.

19

THERE WAS SOMETHING different about him.

She knew it even before he pressed his lips to hers in a kiss that was so soft and reverent that it brought tears to her eyes.

Love.

That's what brought the sudden about-face. He loved her and she loved him.

She *loved* him.

Instead of fighting against the thought, for the first time, she embraced it. Tonight she wanted freedom. From the past. The future. Her insecurities. Her fears.

The realization hit her as she stared up at him and felt the connection flowing between them. She'd never been so in tune with a man.

She'd never wanted to be.

Until now.

He didn't say a word as he picked her up and carried her over to the far corner of the barn where he'd

set up a sleeping bag on a soft mattress of hay. Easing
her down, he shed his jeans and simply stood there,
staring down at her, drinking in the picture she made.

You're so beautiful.

The words echoed in her head and warmth spread
through her, filling up all the gaps and chasing away
the emptiness that had plagued her for so long.

Moonlight pushed through the slats in the wood,
bathing his features in an ethereal glow that made
him almost seem dreamlike.

Almost.

But there was no denying the feel of his hard, hot
body as it stretched out beside hers, or the touch of
his hand as he traced her turgid nipple, or the flutter of his lips as he leaned over and lapped at the
prick points on her breast where he'd drank such a
short time ago.

His tongue laved the sensitive spot and sensation
bolted hot and raw through her. She gasped.

"A bite can be even better than sex," he murmured. To prove his point, he licked her again and
she shuddered. Pleasure drenched her, vibrating
along her nerve endings, stirring her senses until she
wanted him all over again. Here. Now. Everywhere.

She buried her hands in his hair, holding him
close as she arched her breast into the moist heat
of his mouth. He pleasured her, sucking and licking
as one rough fingertip traced the soft folds between
her legs. He pushed inside a delicious fraction and a
gasp bubbled up her throat.

Her body clenched and unclenched around the tip of his finger, desperate to draw him deeper, but he seemed determined to keep things slow and easy.

He smiled, his teeth a startling break in the black shadow of his face. Then the expression faded as he gazed down at her. His attention shifted, traveling from her face, down the column of her neck to her breasts, to the spread of her thighs and his finger, which poised at her pulsing cleft.

He pushed all the way in and she moaned, as pure pleasure pierced her brain. The feeling was so consuming and exquisite that it sucked the air from her lungs. She stopped breathing for a long moment while he held still. Her body settled around him and clamped tighter.

"I want you more than I've ever wanted any woman." *You and only you.*

The words sounded so clear and distinct in her head, so sincere, as if he'd murmured them directly into her ear. He hadn't. He didn't have to. He'd invaded her mind as well as her body, and they were linked now.

Connected.

Forever.

A spurt of excitement went through her. She lifted her pelvis, focusing on the pleasure that gripped her as she worked her body around his decadent finger. She swayed from side to side, her movements frantic, desperate, as she pushed herself higher and higher. She wanted—no, needed—to cram as much as she could into this one moment. To brand his memory into her brain to comfort her on all the lonely nights to come.

Because Shelly Lancaster knew that she would never find another man like Colton Braddock. And it had nothing to do with him being a vampire and everything to do with him being *him*.

He was a man haunted by his past, desperate to make up for it.

They were one and the same.

He'd felt the burden of the world on his shoulders and stepped up to the challenge just the way she had.

But while they'd come from the same place, they'd walked different paths. And those paths were now leading them in very different directions.

While she wanted to hope that he would avenge his family and stay in Skull Creek, she knew deep down inside that such a thing would never happen. While Colton felt convinced the world could never forgive him, the truth was, he couldn't forgive himself.

So all they'd have was tonight.

His mouth swooped down and captured hers in a deep kiss that went way beyond the sweet press of his lips. He coaxed her open and slid his tongue inside to draw on hers for several long moments. Until her frantic heartbeat eased and she forgot all about sucking him deeper into her greedy body.

Instead, she wrapped her arms around him, pulling him even closer and relishing his heartbeat so sure and steady against her own.

A heartbeat?

The question swirled with a dozen others, but she wasn't going to play twenty questions. Or a million, for that matter. This moment was about touching and feeling and *loving*.

He canted his head to the side and deepened the kiss. He plundered her mouth with his, exploring and savoring. The air stalled in her lungs and her heart sped faster. A few more seconds and he tore his mouth from hers.

He slid down her body, now slick from the fever that raged inside of her, and left a blazing path with the velvet tip of his tongue. With a gentle pressure, he parted her thighs. Almost reverently, he stroked the soft, slick folds before settling himself between her legs. His hard, hot length rubbed her pulsing clit for a split-second before he thrust deep and impaled her. Sensation overwhelmed her at first.

She anchored her arms around his neck and her muscles clamped down around his erection. She didn't want to let him go, but he had other ideas.

He withdrew and slid back in for a second time. His hard length rasped her tender insides, creating a delicious friction that sent a dizzying rush straight to her brain. He pulled out again, and went back for a third time. A fourth.

His body pumped into hers over and over, pushing her higher with each delicious plunge. She lifted her hips, meeting him thrust for thrust, eager to feel more of him. Harder. Deeper. Faster.

Look at me. I need to see you. I want to see you.

She opened her eyes at his command to see him poised over her, his gaze bright and gleaming with a purple fire that made her entire body tingle. He pushed into her, his penis hot and twitching, and she knew it was his last and final time.

He let loose a loud hiss that faded into a long moan as Shelly arched her pelvis. His penis throbbed, and she felt a spurt of warmth. He bucked once, twice. His jaw clenched. His mouth fell open and his fangs gleamed in the dim light for a split-second before his mouth closed over the side of her neck where her pulse beat a frantic rhythm and he sank his fangs deep.

Like before, there was no pain. Just a smart prickle followed by a flood of *ohmigod* that drenched her senses and consumed her. A gasp vibrated up her throat. Convulsions gripped her body and suddenly she was floating on a cloud of pure satisfaction.

His mouth eased and he buried his head against her neck as she clung to him, savoring the tremors that rocked them both.

A few frantic heartbeats later, he rolled onto his back, pulling her flush against his side, cradling her as if he never meant to let her go.

But he would.

And she would let him go.

At least that's what she tried to tell herself as she snuggled deeper into his embrace and closed her eyes.

20

"MOTHER GOOSE? This is Little Boy Blue. You copy?"

Bobby's voice pulled Shelly from the oblivion of sleep. She opened her eyes to find sunlight streaming through the slats of the barn.

It was morning.

She sat up and stared around at the massive room, from the far corner where the work bench sat to the rafters overflowing with hay, to the indentation next to her where Colton had been such a short time ago.

He was gone now.

Duh.

It was daylight and he was a vampire and—

The thought stalled as the images from the past night rushed at her.

The hayride.

Honey's near breakdown.

The high speed chase.

The apprehension.

The truth.

The sex.

She touched a hand to her neck, but the prick points had already disappeared, leaving only a sensitive patch of skin that tingled when she touched it. Her thighs ached and her body felt limp and tired.

And she loved it.

She stretched out and basked in the afterglow of their incredible lovemaking for the next few moments, until Bobby's voice crackled in the air again, telling her that she wasn't alone.

Oh, no.

She bolted to her feet and snatched up the discarded dress. Her coat was back at the road and the only thing she had was a miniscule slip of spandex. She was practically naked and someone from the Sheriff's office was outside.

Panic bolted through her and she snatched up the sleeping bag, draping it securely over her shoulders as she walked to the barn door and peered out to see the cruiser just outside.

Dread rushed through her, followed by a rush of relief when she realized that it was *her* cruiser and the voice was coming from the police band radio drifting through the open windows.

"Mama Goose? You copy?"

She hiked the sleeping bag tighter and walked out into the sunlight. Climbing in, she grabbed the radio. "What happened to Mama Bear?"

"Shelly? Is that you?"

"Last time I looked."

"Thank God. I was starting to get worried. I know a busted pipe can take awhile, but you haven't even called in and you *always* call in and—"

"Busted pipe?"

"That security guy left a message that you two decided to go over some specs last night. He said your pipe busted and you were busy trying to keep the downstairs from flooding which is why you didn't answer our calls. Haven't you found a plumber yet? I told you my brother-in-law can take a look..." Bobby droned on while Shelly fixated on the truth.

Colton Braddock had retrieved her car. And her coat, she realized as she glanced at the pile of wool sitting on the seat next to her. And he'd called in for her. Just like he'd picked her up last night when they'd heard the car approaching and high-tailed it to the privacy of the old barn.

Because he loved her.

She knew it. At the same time, he hadn't actually said the words.

Maybe he'd only picked up the pieces to preserve her reputation so she could go back to her life and he could get on with his.

Probably.

Disappointment ricocheted through her and she shook it away. She should be thankful. Her job meant everything.

Then and now.

One night of hot sex couldn't change that. Even if it had been the best of her life.

"I'm still working on getting a plumber," she told Bobby. "I'll check in later." She hooked the radio receiver in place and keyed the engine. Her gaze stalled on the barn and she had half a mind to head back inside and look for him. He was there somewhere. Hidden away from the sunlight. From her.

But what would she say?

Don't go.

Let's work it out.

I love you.

Crazy.

She shoved the car into reverse and swung the cruiser around. Gravel spewed and brakes squealed.

It's not like she'd thought for even five seconds that they might have a future together. That he could make peace with his past and she could forget hers, and they could both live happily ever after.

Okay, so maybe five seconds.

But that had been in the throes of passion, with lust clouding her judgment. Now, she was sitting smack dab in the middle of the bright light of day, reality blaring in her head.

He was a vampire. She was a human. He thrived on blood and sex. She preferred a good cheeseburger and a milkshake. He crashed during the day and thrived at night. She worked seven to seven and slept like a baby in between.

They were polar opposites. It could never work even if they wanted it to.

Which they didn't.

He didn't.

That was why she had to push last night completely out of her mind, get her act together and get back to work.

Because when Colton Braddock finally faced his past and gave up his life, that's all she would have left.

If only the realization didn't make her want to forget all about work, head home, crawl into bed and cry her eyes out.

SHE FORGOT ABOUT work, headed home, crawled into bed and cried her eyes out.

For a little while.

But then reality intruded. Bobby's brother-in-law showed up on her doorstep to fix her non-existent broken pipe. Darla called about a zillion times to say that Tom had cornered her the night before and they'd slept together. The *Gazette* sent over a copy of the retraction for her approval. Life moved on, and Shelly had to move with it.

Colton Braddock was history.

That's what she told herself as she dragged herself out from under the covers, pulled on her uniform and headed to the office.

"Yes, I'm wearing lipstick," she told John when she walked into work just after lunch. "And blush. And mascara. And a LOT of concealer." She'd been desperate to hide her tired eyes and the sadness that roiled inside of her. "Now put your eyes back in your head and get to work."

Oddly enough, they did just that and Shelly had the fleeting thought that Colton was right. Maybe she didn't have to hide who she really was in order to keep everyone's respect.

She drop-kicked the thought the minute it struck. She wasn't going to think about him. And she certainly wasn't going to worry about him. Or the fact that he was *this* close to facing off with the vampire who'd murdered his family and there wasn't a damned thing she could do to help him.

She had no clue when Rose Braddock would show up, where the confrontation would take place or even when it was going to happen.

A wave of helplessness rolled through her and just like that, she was hiding under the bed, scared and powerless and so very afraid.

Before she could dwell on the realization, Bobby walked in and dumped a major distraction into her lap.

"Honey missed her court date this morning and Judge Myers is about to issue a warrant for her arrest." He headed for the weapons cabinet that sat against the far wall. "I explained the situation, but he's pissed because you went over his head. He says if we don't have her in his office by the end of the day, he's going to call Sheriff Keller and have you suspended."

Uh-oh. "Did you go by her place?"

"First thing. I knocked for about forty-five minutes. I think she's inside, but I have no way of knowing for sure. That's why I came back here." He punched in the security code for the cabinet and the lock clicked. He snatched up several three-inch long cylinders and stuffed them into his shirt pocket and closed the cabinet. The lock clicked. "If she won't come out on her own, I'll just have to gas her out."

"Oh, no you won't." Shelly was right behind him, plucking the cylinders from his pocket. She stuffed them into her pants. Honey might be breaking the law by resisting, but she was no criminal. She was a woman. A stressed out, sexually frustrated woman who was probably terrified at the thought of ending up back in the cell across from Holbrook. She was probably buried under the covers right now, hiding from the world, crying her eyes out. "I'll go get her."

"But—"

"We just got a call from Mr. Rigsby out on Route 9." She handed him the call sheet. "His horse is missing and he needs help finding it."

"You get to have all the fun," he grumbled as he took the sheet and headed back out the door.

Fifteen minutes later, Shelly pulled up outside the small beige house with yellow trim that sat on the east side of town. The yard was about the size of a postage stamp with hedges lining the perimeter. Daisies poured out of the window box near the front door. The light on the porch flickered. Once. Twice.

"Honey, I know you're in there." Shelly knocked on the door. "Open up."

Somewhere inside, Blake Shelton sang about honey bees. A mixer *whirred*. Pots and pans clanged.

"I know you're upset, but hiding isn't going to solve anything. You missed your court date this morning and my ass is on the line."

"I'm sorry." She heard a frustrated voice from inside. "I really am, but I just can't do it."

"You won't have to go near the jail or Holbrook. I promise."

"I still can't go," Honey called out. More pans rattled. "Please don't be mad at me."

Shelly remembered the small cylinders stuffed into her pocket. "I've got tear gas." Not that she was about to use it, but Honey didn't know that. "I'll use it. I swear—"

Hinges rattled and the door swung open. Honey stood framed in the doorway, a flour-stained àpron that read *Kiss My Cupcakes* wrapped around her waist. Cake batter smudged one cheek and a clump of white frosting stuck in her hair.

"I'll go straight to the courthouse first thing tomorrow morning," she said, hiking a massive mixing bowl onto one hip. "Cross my heart. I just have to get these cupcakes done first." She stuck her finger in the bowl and licked a dab of chocolate. Determination fired her eyes. "I have to."

Obviously the donuts hadn't been enough to curb

her frustration. She'd gone off the deep end. Straight into a vat of cupcakes.

"You don't have to do this," Shelly told her.

Frustration edged Honey's voice and she nodded. "Yes, I do. I don't have a choice."

"Listen, I know exactly how you feel." The hopelessness. The desperation. Shelly felt both. She didn't stand a chance with Colton. At the same time, she wanted one. "But you don't have to give in to your weaknesses. Don't do it," Shelly said, as much for herself as for Honey. "Don't chuck it all for a little instant gratification. You've worked too hard to get here. He isn't worth it. Holbrook is a criminal. A bad guy. You deserve better."

Honey looked surprised. "I'm not doing this for Jimmy. Landsakes, I haven't even given him a second thought since last night."

"But you were hooked on him."

She shrugged. "I know, but then I came home and I got busy and suddenly he was history." Her attention shifted back to the mixing bowl. "This is for the steer."

Honey's words punched the rewind button on Shelly's memory and reminded her about the steer made of cupcakes being unveiled at the finals for the chili cook-off of Thursday.

"That's tonight, isn't it?"

"Eight o'clock sharp." Panic lit the woman's eyes. "I either deliver on time or I'm out two thousand dollars in commission and the advertising opportunity of a lifetime." A buzzer went off and the lights flickered again. "My mixers," she said. "I've got too many plugged into one outlet. They're overloading my circuits. But a girl's gotta do what a girl's gotta do, right? Hold this." She thrust the mixing bowl at Shelly. "I'll be right back."

A few heartbeats later, the buzzer went silent and the lights stop flickering.

"Don't just stand there," Honey called from inside. "Come on in."

Shelly followed the sugary sweet smell of freshly baked goodies to the kitchen in time to see Honey pull a massive baking sheet laden with fifty cupcakes from one of the three ovens crammed into the small room. Her gaze shifted to the chicken wire monstrosity taking up most of the room. Cupcakes covered half the sculpture making up the animal's head and torso, while the rest sat waiting for Honey to work her magic.

"I call him Bubba," Honey said, reaching for two jumbo cupcakes sitting on a nearby cooling rack. "You're just in time to help me do his testicles."

"I think I'll pass."

"Don't be such a wuss. It's just flour and sugar." Desperation gleamed in her eyes as she held out a spare apron. "Come on. I could really use an extra set of hands. I'll even let you lick the bowls," she added, trying to tip the scales in her favor.

Shelly thought of the alternative—an entire day sitting at her desk, eating stale donuts, worrying over

Colton and the all-important fact that she loved him and he didn't love her back. Life totally sucked.

Or an entire day spent baking—and eating—a gazillion home-made cupcakes.

She wrapped the apron around her waist, rolled up her sleeves and reached for the two massive cupcakes. "Let's give Bubba something to be proud of."

21

SHE WAS EARLY.

Colton opened his eyes to the shadowy interior of the barn and the unsettling truth zipping up and down his spine.

Awareness sizzled along his nerve endings, more intense than the steady buzz he usually felt from his brothers and the Skull Creek Chopper vampires. No, this was different. This was Rose.

Shit.

The sun was about to set and twilight filled the old barn. Colton pushed aside the wall of hay bales surrounding him and climbed to his feet. He ducked his way past the rafters that criss-crossed the ceiling and headed for the edge of the loft. He leaped to the barn floor in one smooth movement that didn't so much as stir the dust beneath his bare feet. He walked over to the far corner and pulled jeans and a T-shirt from his duffel bag. Next, he yanked on his boots, his movements quick, desperate.

Early of all things.

Brent's calculations had been wrong. His brother had estimated they would have at least one more day before Rose showed up in Skull Creek. Plenty of time for Colton to see Shelly again and pour out his heart.

If that had been his plan.

It wasn't.

One more day or fifty, it made little difference. He would never go after her and confess his love. It was over between them and so he had to let her go.

He wanted her to go.

His gaze hooked on the piece of cedar he'd been working on the night before and before he could stop himself, he crossed the room and touched the smooth piece of wood. Shelly's image stirred and he felt the press of her body against his back, her delicate hands resting atop his, her warmth seeping clear into his bones as she'd talked about her past and he'd told her about his.

Warm. For the first time in one hundred and fifty years.

Pure joy leaped through him because he'd finally found the one thing that made him feel whole again. It was followed by a bolt of anger because he didn't deserve it.

He'd messed up. He'd failed his brothers. His son.

Especially his son. And while he took some comfort in the fact that CJ had escaped the torture of a bullet, it did little to ease the knot in his chest. His son had grown up without a father.

His body tightened and his muscles jumped. In a flash, he snatched up the cedar and threw it as far as he could. The wood slammed into the ground and split into two. It was done.

Over.

He grabbed his duffel bag and unearthed the two deadly looking stakes he'd carved himself the night he'd gotten the phone call from Cody telling him the truth about Rose. That she was guilty. That Colton was finally going to get his shot at revenge.

Two matching stakes.

One for the traitor who'd destroyed his family. And one for himself, because when all was said and done, he'd let them down even more than Rose.

He stiffened. Those days were over. He couldn't change the past, but he could keep it from ever happening again.

The sweet smell of cupcakes tickled his nostrils and he stiffened. *Shelly.* Thanks to last night, they were really and truly connected now. She was thinking about him. Worrying over him. Wanting him, despite making up her mind that she wasn't going to do either.

He knew the feeling, but it would end soon.

She would be free and so would he.

That's what he told himself. If only freedom didn't look like an even bigger hell than the one he'd existed in all of these years.

Forcing aside the notion, he shoved the stakes back into his bag and walked out to his truck. Climbing behind the wheel, he keyed the engine, backed out of the driveway and headed into town.

While he would never act on the feelings for Shelly pushing and pulling inside of him, he still felt them. He couldn't let her get caught in the cross-fire because of his own desperate need for revenge.

He wouldn't.

Rose was close. Headed straight to the Sheriff's office. Which meant Colton had to get Holbrook out of there and move him before all hell broke loose and Shelly ended up smack dab in the middle of it all.

As he rolled past, his gaze stalled on the old, aban-doned farmhouse that reminded him so much of the Circle B. It would be the perfect place for him to face off with Rose. To avenge his family and doom her the way she'd doomed them all.

And then?

And then nothing. He would destroy her, and then he would pay for his own sins the way he'd always meant to.

Fighting down a wave of regret, he slammed his foot down on the gas and gunned the engine. The hair on the back of his neck prickled and his nerves buzzed as he sped down the dirt road.

She was getting closer, all right, and the clock was ticking.

AFTER AN ENTIRE DAY spent baking and frosting cup-cakes, Shelly had learned a few things about herself. First, she wasn't half bad when it came to baking—

they'd only had to pull out the fire extinguisher once. Two, she preferred Swiss chocolate mocha cake batter over vanilla bean. And three, she would never be able to forget Colton Braddock.

She didn't want to forget.

She wanted to find him, help him, love him. Regardless of the fact that they were polar opposites. Or that he was a vampire. Or that this wasn't the right time in her life for her to get her very own happily ever after.

Everything was all wrong and yet it had never felt so right.

Up until about an hour ago, that is.

That's when she'd started to feel the panic and anxiety and fear. Not her own, but Colton's. Something was happening and she could only pray that she wasn't too late.

She hurried up the steps of the massive house with its white columns and perfectly shaped hedges. Before she could press the bell, the door flew open and she found herself staring at none other than Cody "Balls to the wall" Braddock.

He had dark hair, striking silver eyes and the muscular physique befitting that of a badass pro bull rider. He'd been the best of the best up until last year when he'd retired to settle down and marry one of Skull Creek's own.

Shelly could have sworn she saw a flicker of surprise when his gaze collided with hers. But then his mouth pulled into a tight line that said he wasn't the least bit pleased.

"You know about us." As if his words had conjured them, Travis and Brent stepped from the shadows and flanked her on either side.

She glanced at both men and nodded. "I also know what's coming and I want to help. But I can't do that without details. I need to know when, where, how—"

"Cody? Why is everyone still standing out here…" The words faded as Miranda Braddock came up behind her husband. She stared past him. "Deputy Lancaster," she said, obviously startled. "I didn't know you were here."

"I'm surprised you didn't sense me."

A smile touched Miranda's lips and her eyes gleamed with an unearthly light that Shelly recognized all too well. "I'm still new at this. Besides, you aren't the only human in the bunch. I thought you were Abby." She motioned to the petite brunette who stepped up next to Brent. "Or Holly." The town's local wedding planner joined Travis and slid her hand into his.

"Not that the situation is permanent," Abby chimed in, eyeing Brent. "We just thought we'd save a little something for the wedding night."

"That's right," Holly chimed in. "'Til death do us part isn't nearly long enough when you love someone."

A pang of envy shot through Shelly, but it faded in the next heartbeat when her gut tightened again and a wave of anxiety hit her. "Please." She eyed Cody. "We don't have much time."

"She wants to know about Rose," he told Miranda when she shot him a questioning glance.

"Well go on, then. She needs to know. She obviously loves him."

"Did you just read my mind?"

Miranda smiled. "I didn't have to, sweetie." She turned and motioned Shelly to follow her inside. "It's written all over your face."

"I WAS WONDERING when someone was going to finally let me out of here," Jimmy Holbrook declared when Colton pulled on leather gloves, gripped the door and slid it to the side.

"The redhead?" Colton pulled off the gloves that were now smoking, tossed them to the side and eyed the young man who reached for his shirt.

Jimmy shrugged. "Red hair, brown hair, purple hair—it makes no never mind. A friendly smile and just like that, somebody's lending a helping hand."

He didn't know about Rose.

Colton saw as much blazing in the man's familiar blue eyes. Forget Rose and her vamp charisma. Jimmy thought it was his own easy charm that had persuaded that guard back in Houston to open the door. His quick grin that had lured the police officer up in Austin into forgetting to lock the handcuffs.

The young man had no clue he had a self-appointed guardian angel, one who was on par with the devil himself.

"What are you doing?" Jimmy demanded when Colton grabbed a wrist and snapped a handcuff around it.

"I'm not letting you out."

"What—"

"You're being transferred." Before the young man knew what was coming, Colton pulled his arm behind his back and went for the other hand.

"What about Ranger Truitt? I thought he was riding shotgun during the transfer."

"He's been replaced." Colton snapped the second cuff into place and shoved Jimmy toward the cell door. "Now move."

If SHELLY HADN'T already been hopelessly in love with Colton Braddock, she would have surely fallen head over heels after hearing the Braddocks talk about their oldest brother.

Colton had been a loyal, kind, caring man who'd sacrificed everything for his family. That's why Rose's treachery had been so devastating.

The woman had not only turned her back on her husband, she'd killed her own son.

Shelly couldn't begin to grasp how someone could do such a thing to their own flesh and blood, anymore than she could understand how her own mother had turned her back time and time again. But people did bad things all the time. She'd learned that much during her ten years with the department. It was a screwed up world.

Especially for one loyal, trusting cowboy who'd given everything for his family.

As she listened to the story of that night and the years that followed, she gained a new appreciation for the pain and grief that ate away at Colton Braddock. The anger that drove him. The demons that haunted him.

His entire existence was hinged on finding the traitor and punishing her. And now it was about to happen. The Braddock Brothers had found her weakness and lured her to Skull Creek, using her last living descendant as bait.

Jimmy Holbrook.

"I have to get back to the office," Shelly blurted as the truth gripped her as tightly as the fear coiling in her gut.

"We'll go, too—" Cody said, but the radio clipped to Shelly's collar buzzed and Bobby's voice filled her ears.

"Shelly? You need to get back here," the deputy said in a frantic voice. "We've got a serious situation."

"I know. I need you lock down the entire jail and don't let anyone in or out—"

"Holbrook's gone," he blurted. "One minute he was here and the next, he just disappeared. We don't know what the hell happened. Truitt is about to have a friggin' conniption."

Cody exchanged glances with his brothers. "Rose," the three men said in unison, but Shelly knew better.

She knew the truth.

She could feel it pumping through her veins.

The fear.

The anxiety.

The relief.

Because Colton had managed to get Holbrook away from the jail.

"It's Colton. He took him."

"Why?" Cody asked, but Shelly already knew the answer to that. He wanted Shelly safe.

The realization sent a burst of warmth through her, followed by a rush of panic so profound that tears burned the backs of her eyes. Because she knew what was coming. She could feel it.

"Where do you think they went?" Brent asked, but she already knew the answer to that, as well.

She smelled the musky scent of rotting wood and stale air and realization struck.

The farmhouse.

The minute the truth hit her, she knew Colton had read the thought, as well. She felt him stiffen. And then, just like that, the connection severed and there was nothing.

No fear. No expectancy. No Colton.

No!

"I've got to get out of here." She left the brothers staring after her as she turned and bolted for her cruiser.

"We'll go with you," Cody called behind her, but she refused to slow down.

She couldn't.

She'd already wasted enough time. Too much. And now all she could do was pray as she hit gas and headed hell for leather down the dirt road.

Please don't let it be too late.

22

HE'D BEEN WAITING for this moment for one hundred and fifty years.

Colton stood in the shadows off to the side of the house and watched as Rose Braddock stepped up onto the decrepit porch, moving toward the open doorway and the man tied to a chair just a few feet inside.

Clouds had moved in, making the night blacker than ever, but Colton didn't need any help seeing the woman who'd taken everything from him.

She looked exactly as he remembered. Same determined set to her jaw. Same small, petite frame. Her red hair had been pulled back into a tight ponytail. She wore black jeans, a black T-shirt and black high-heeled boots. Her steps were slow, tentative, as if she knew someone was watching her.

Or following her.

She glanced over her shoulder, her gaze scanning the road that she'd just driven down, before she seemed to conquer her fears. She turned back to the house and disappeared inside.

Colton reached the doorway a split-second later.

He watched as she approached the young man who sat there, his arms and legs fastened to the chair, his head drooping down, a steady snore flaring his nostrils, totally oblivious to what was going on, thanks to Colton. She didn't bend down and try to wake him or untie his ropes. She stalled, standing there for a long moment before her familiar voice echoed off the walls.

"You're going to kill me."

She turned and Colton found himself face-to-face with his past. Rage welled up inside him and his body shook with the force of it. "Payback's a bitch," he growled.

He had her by the throat in that next instant. He flew through the air, slamming her back against a far wall. Wood buckled and split and she went sprawling backward into the next room.

Colton was on her in a heartbeat, the stake in his hand, fury gripping him from head to toe. His vision clouded and suddenly everything went a bright red. He lifted his arm, but he didn't send the stake plunging into her heart. Not yet. His hand stalled.

Because as much as he needed to send her straight to hell where she belonged, he needed something else even more at that moment.

"Why did you do it?" He voiced the one question that had eaten away at him for so long.

He didn't think she would answer at first. She simply stared up at him, into him, and he feared that she would hurt him one last and final time by denying him the answer he so desperately sought.

"I never loved you," she finally said. "You knew that." If he hadn't known better, he would have sworn she seemed almost sad about that fact. Regretful.

But he knew better. He knew her.

What she was capable of.

The deceit. The pain. The death.

"I wanted more than a ranch out in the middle of nowhere," she continued. "I wanted to live in town and wear fancy dresses and be somebody other than a bastard's daughter or a rancher's wife." She shook her head.

"Why not just leave?" His fingers tightened on her arm, but she didn't so much as flinch. As if she didn't feel the pain. As if she deserved it. "You didn't have to do what you did. You didn't have to kill them all."

"That wasn't my idea. I thought we were just going to pick up and go. That's what Jacob said.... He said we could take CJ with us and we'd go someplace new. Some place exciting."

"Jacob?" Colton's mind stuck on the name. "Jacob Manning?" The man had been the ranch foreman at the Circle B for ten years. He'd been there that night. He'd died there. "He was the man you left with?"

She nodded. "After you left, we started having an affair. Time's were tight, but he managed to buy me pretty dresses and he made all the right promises. I was so gullible." She shook her head. "I believed him."

"I thought he died that night."

"That's what he wanted everyone to think. That it was an Apache attack. He said we had to do it. That if we didn't, someone would come after us. I didn't want to, but he did it anyway."

"And you were completely innocent, right?"

"No." She shook her head. "I was even more guilty than he was. I let him." She shook her head. "I watched him set the fire and I didn't do a single thing to stop him. I saw what he was capable of that night. That's why I didn't keep CJ with me. I left him at the first town we reached, before I was turned. He deserved something better than me, and a hell of a lot better than Jacob." She closed her eyes. "He's a sadistic bastard." Her gaze locked with Colton's. "I tried leaving him years ago, but he won't let me go. He keeps coming after me and it's all I can do to stay one step ahead of him." Anguish gleamed in her eyes. "He'd be here right now if he knew about Jimmy, but luckily he doesn't. Not yet. I've managed to keep this one secret all these years, but I know he'll catch up to me eventually. And then he'll punish me by taking the one thing I have left."

Colton knew then that Rose was already in a hell far worse than any he could doom her to. She was trapped for eternity with a vampire she hated. A slave to her mistakes. Her past.

She'd kept going all these years, not for her own

selfish reasons, but for their son. For CJ's descendants. For Holbrook.

"But you're here now," she said, a small smile touching her lips. "You can look out for him." And then, before he knew what was happening, she grabbed his hand and lunged toward him.

The stake sunk deep, impaling her, and her entire body started to shake. Smoke steamed from the wound and just like that, her body crumpled, fading into a pile of ashes at Colton's feet.

Rose was truly, finally, dead.

The realization didn't bring nearly the rush of satisfaction that he'd expected. He staggered back a few feet, the past whirling inside him as he turned and reached for his duffel bag. She was dead, but it wasn't over. She hadn't been the only one to blame for that night.

He pulled out the second stake.

"Don't!" The frantic voice rang out a split-second before Shelly grabbed him from behind. The motion caught him off guard and he found himself flat on his back, her knee on his chest, her face looming over his. "You can't do this. I won't let you do it."

"They're dead because of me."

"No one blames you." She eyed him. "Except for you. They've all forgiven you, Colton, but you have to forgive yourself."

She was right. He knew that as his brothers stepped up behind her. He could see the truth shining in their eyes. The acceptance. The love.

They were family. They would always be a family.

"There's been enough death," Brent said. *"Enough."*

"It's time to let it go," Shelly added, reading the turmoil in his eyes, feeling it in his heart. They were one now. The bond unbreakable. Forged in blood and sex and love. Especially love. "I love you, too," she added. "So don't do this. Please." Panic filled her gaze. "If you do, you'll just be hurting me the way that Rose hurt you all those years ago."

"I would never hurt you."

She eyed the stake and challenge gleamed in her gaze. "Then prove it."

He couldn't. This was his last chance to lay the past to rest. To find peace.

But suddenly, he knew there would be no peace in death. Not if he left Shelly. He would feel nothing, but she would be here dealing with the aftermath. Hurt. Devastated.

While he didn't know if he could ever forgive himself the way his brothers had, suddenly he wanted to try.

Wood clattered to the floor. "It won't be easy," he warned. "You. Me. There are going to be lots of complications."

"We'll work through them. Isn't that what people in love do?"

"That's exactly what they do," Cody said.

"Hell, yeah," Brent chimed in.

"You're preaching to the choir, bro," added Travis.

Colton grinned and eyed the woman standing in

front of him. She was so strong. So stubborn. So beautiful. "You're something else, you know that?"

"Something good, I hope."

"Something wonderful." He hauled her close. "I love you. I'll always love you."

"Always is an awful long time."

"I'm a vampire, remember? I've got all the time in the world." And then Colton hauled her close, kissed her for all he was worth, and just like that, he found the peace he'd been praying for all these years.

Epilogue

Two months later...

"THERE'S NO SENSE arguing about this," Shelly told Colton. "I've got my mind made up."

"Don't I get any sort of say so?"

"About this? No." She stared at the man she loved more than anything in the entire world. He perched on one knee on the porch in front of her, a frustrated expression on his face, a very large, very beautiful two carat diamond ring in his hand.

It wasn't exactly a surprise at this point. They'd been living together, loving each other and so she'd seen this coming a long time ago. Colton had taken on Jimmy Holbrook at his cattle ranch in New Mexico as part of a work-release program. If the young man kept up his end of the bargain and worked his ass off, the place would one day be his. In the meantime, he was answering to Colton's tough-as-nails foreman who didn't take crap from anyone. And he was probably hating every minute of it.

But the young man was learning.

Meanwhile, Colton had moved to Skull Creek to settle down with his family. With her.

He'd been ready to take things slow with his brothers, convinced that the years apart had done irreparable damage to their relationship, but determined to try anyway.

But he was fast learning that love had a way of overcoming all obstacles. He was as close as ever to his brothers and had just purchased the two hundred acres that sat next to Brent's property. While the Circle B had been their family's legacy once upon a time, the brothers had overcome their past and were now building a new legacy right here in Skull Creek.

Colton had finally made his peace and now it was time to take the next step. They'd come outside to sit and enjoy the warm summer evening and he'd dropped down on one knee and popped the question.

"Will you marry me?"

She'd wanted to scream *yes* and shout it from the rooftops, but there was still the little matter of Colton being a vampire and Shelly being a human to consider. And while she knew that his brothers had married humans that they would eventually turn when the time was right, Shelly was ready now.

When she pulled on her Grandma Jean's wedding dress and walked down the aisle and said, "I do," she wanted to mean it. No more demons from the past standing between them. No more secrets. No more walls.

No more fear.

"I want this," she told him. "I want you."

"And here I thought you were just using me for my powers." He slipped the ring onto her finger and settled down next to her on the custom-made bench he'd given her just last week. They'd set it up on the front porch and had been using it every night since. "Not that you need another dose of badass. You've got plenty of your own. You'll make one hell of a Sheriff anyway, come the fall."

She shook her head. "I know we've come out of the dark ages with free wifi at the café, but I don't think Skull Creek is ready for a vampire Sheriff just yet."

"I don't know about that. Everybody seems to like Sheriff Keller."

Her gaze collided with his. "Are you trying to tell me that Matt is a vampire?"

"Not exactly. He's half werewolf and half vampire, so he can walk around during the day. But the full moon's a bitch." His gaze touched hers. "If he can do it, you can, too. Don't give up on your dream because of me."

She smiled. "You are my dream."

He settled down next to her for the next few moments as she thought about the past.

Jason Aldean drifted from the radio singing about

green tractors and taking a ride and Colton pushed to his feet. He held out a hand. "Dance with me?"

"Right here?" Her gaze slid to the old lady who stood across the street, watering her grass. She kept glancing at them, obviously waiting to see what would happen next so she could get on the phone and call somebody in her bridge group, who'd call somebody from Bingo, who'd tell somebody from church and so on, until the entire town new that Shelly Lancaster was dancing on her front porch.

Dancing, of all things.

With the man she loved.

She let Colton pull her to her feet and a split second later, she was in his arms and they were swaying to the slow country tune.

And there wasn't a place in the world that she would rather be. She loved Colton and he loved her and nothing else mattered.

* * * * *

PASSION

Harlequin® Blaze

COMING NEXT MONTH
AVAILABLE JUNE 26, 2012

#693 LEAD ME HOME
Sons of Chance
Vicki Lewis Thompson
Matthew Tredway has made a name for himself as a world-class horse trainer. Only, after one night with Aurelia Smith, he's the one being led around by the nose....

#694 THE GUY MOST LIKELY TO...
A Blazing Hot Summer Read
Leslie Kelly, Janelle Denison and Julie Leto
Every school has one. That special guy, the one every girl had to have or they'd just die! Did you ever wonder what happened to him? Come back to school with three of Blaze's bestselling authors and find out how great the nights are after the glory days are over....

#695 TALL, DARK & RECKLESS
Heather MacAllister
After interviewing a thousand men, dating coach Piper Scott knows handsome daredevil foreign journalist Mark Banning is definitely not her type—but what if he's her perfect man?

#696 NO HOLDS BARRED
Forbidden Fantasies
Cara Summers
Defense attorney Piper MacPherson is being threatened by a stalker and protected by FBI profiler Duncan Sutherland. Her problem? She's not sure which is more dangerous....

#697 BREATHLESS ON THE BEACH
Flirting with Justice
Wendy Etherington
When PR exec Victoria Holmes attends a client's beach-house party, she has no idea there'll be cowboys—well, one cowboy. Lucky for Victoria, Jarred McKenna's not afraid to get a little wet....

#698 NO GOING BACK
Uniformly Hot!
Karen Foley
Army Special Ops commando Chase Rawlins has been trained to handle anything. Only, little does he guess how much he'll enjoy "handling" sexy publicist Kate Fitzgerald!

New York Times *and* USA TODAY *bestselling author
Vicki Lewis Thompson returns with yet another irresistible
cowpoke! Meet Mathew Tredway—cowboy, horse
whisperer and honorary Son of Chance.*

Read on for a sneak peek from the bestselling miniseries
SONS OF CHANCE:

LEAD ME HOME
Available July 2012 only from Harlequin® Blaze™.

AS MATTHEW RETURNED to the corral and Houdini, the
taste of Aurelia's mouth was on his lips and her scent clung
to his clothes. He'd briefly satisfied the craving growing
within him, and like a light snack before a meal, it would
have to do.

When he'd first walked into the kitchen, his mind had
been occupied with the challenge of training Houdini. He'd
thought his concentration would hold long enough to get
some carrots, ask about the corn bread and leave before
succumbing to Aurelia's appeal. He'd miscalculated. Within
a very short time, desire had claimed every brain cell.

Although seducing her this morning was out of the question, his libido had demanded some sort of satisfaction.
He'd tried to deny that urge and had nearly made it out of
the house. Apparently his willpower was no match for the
temptation of Aurelia's mouth, though, and he'd turned
around.

If he'd ever felt this kind of desperate need for a woman,
he couldn't recall it. During the night, as he'd lain in his
narrow bunk listening to the cowhands snore, he'd searched
for an explanation as to why Aurelia affected him this way.

Sometime in the early-morning hours he'd come up with

the answer. After years of dating women who were rolling stones like he was, he'd developed an itch for a hearth-and-home kind of woman. Aurelia, with her cooking skills and voluptuous body, could give him that.

With luck, once he'd scratched this particular itch, he'd be fine again. He certainly hoped so, because he had no intention of giving up his career, and travel was a built-in requirement. Plus he liked to travel and had no real desire to stay in one spot and become domesticated.

Tonight he'd say all that to Aurelia, because he didn't want her going into this with any illusions about permanence. He figured that when the right guy came along, she'd get married and have kids.

Too bad that guy wouldn't be him....

Will Aurelia be the one to corral this cowboy for good?
Find out in: LEAD ME HOME

Available July 2012
wherever Harlequin® Blaze™ books are sold.

This summer, celebrate everything Western
with Harlequin® Books!

www.Harlequin.com/Western

HBEXP0712